At First Blush

DAWN FITZPATRICK #1 OF THE IMMORTELLE SERIES

Second Edition (v2.1)

Dedication

To Igor. You proved that the right word at the right moment can save a life – or a book. Thank you.

.

Abigail Hawk

THE IMMORTELLE SERIES
The Immortality Clause (Claudia Bell #1)
At First Blush (Dawn Fitzpatrick #1)
Love Thy Enemy (Anya Karekanova #1)
Beneath The Dragon Sun (Anya Karekanova #2)
The Traitor's Web (Anya Karekanova #3)

V. L. Dreyer

THE SURVIVORS
The Survivors Book I: Summer
The Survivors Book II: Autumn
The Survivors Book III: Winter
The Survivors Book IV: Spring

Prologue

Cijal gazed in wonder at the tiny girl playing on the seashore. He could tell she was a girl because her long, curly hair and delicate features spoke of things feminine, but her overall appearance was completely alien. Her skin was a soft shade of pink dusted with tiny brown spots, and her hair was a rich, deep reddish-orange, like the crystals that formed around the edge of the hot pools at home. He'd never seen anyone like her.

She was about his age, maybe a little bit younger. Though he knew that his mother would be angry with him, he was fascinated by the girl and wanted to watch a while longer. She was chasing something across the compacted sand. It was a tiny crab, small and agile, and it had no trouble escaping from her curious fingers.

Why is she chasing it? he wondered. *Does she want to eat it? Surely it would be easier to catch something trapped in the tide pools.*

Cijal eased himself up a little to get a better look at the crab. No, it was much too small to eat. Was she chasing it for pleasure, then? For fun? That he could understand; he often chased small fish or crustaceans for the very same reason, to see what the tiny creatures would do when threatened. But, more importantly, where were the adults?

He looked up and down the shoreline but saw no sign of them. There must have been some nearby, he reasoned. She was much too young to live by herself.

Cijal had learned about the humans at school, and he knew they lived in family groups much like his own people. She would have a mother and father somewhere, perhaps brothers and sisters as well.

Maybe her parents don't know where she is, he thought. *Perhaps she snuck away to explore, like me.*

That piqued his interest. Curiosity had driven him towards the shore, hoping to catch sight of one of the mysterious humans. His mother would *never* have approved. According to his parents and teachers, anything that lived on the land was a danger to him. Both the mortals and immortals alike were vicious predators that would kill him – or worse.

The little girl didn't look like a predator, though. She was so tiny she hardly even posed a threat to the crab.

Suddenly, the fleeing crab made a misstep, and the little girl caught it quite by accident. She looked just as shocked as the crab must have been and froze in her tracks, then she dropped the crab with a high-pitched squeal and danced away from it.

The child's cry brought an immediate response from the structure up on the hill. An adult female emerged and called down to the girl in a language Cijal didn't understand. The human child called something back and laughed gleefully. Cijal grinned to himself; while their languages and looks were completely different, the sound of their laughter was just the same.

Apparently content that her offspring was in no real danger, the adult female vanished back into the structure on the hill. Cijal was even more fascinated now; the adult female had pale pink skin and red-orange hair, just like the girl. For an adult and child to look so similar seemed very strange to him. His appearance was different to that of his parents, and he would not start to take on his adult colours until puberty. Right now, he was only six years old, and that seemed like an eternity away.

He shot a wary glance back over his shoulder at the open ocean, using all of his innate senses to search for any signs of danger, but there were none. All was quiet and still, except for the little girl playing on the shore. Her curls bounced across her shoulders as she scampered down the beach, heading right for the tide-pools where he was hiding.

He froze, fearing that she'd spotted him despite his natural camouflage, but she ran right past him to one of the smaller pools a few meters to his right.

What's she doing now? he wondered

Overcome by curiosity, he crept a few inches closer to get a better look. She appeared to be poking the tide-pool with one finger. Poke, poke, poke. He lifted his head, just a little bit, enough to see what the girl was doing. She was using her index finger to prod tiny sea-anemones, and watching with intense fascination when they closed up to hide their soft interiors. Cijal couldn't help but laugh.

The girl's head jerked up, and she stared right at him with wide eyes. He ducked behind a rock but it was far too late – she'd seen right through his camouflage, because he'd made the foolish mistake of giving himself away. He heard her calling out to him, but he was already fleeing. Everything he'd been told about the humans warned him that they were dangerous, even that harmless-looking girl-child.

Too frightened to stop, Cijal darted down into the depths and swam away as fast as he could, retreating back to the safety of the underwater caves where his family lived.

***

"Wait! Come back, boy!"

The girl called, scampering down to the ocean's edge, but the phantom child in the ocean was gone. She watched the waves for a long time after that, trying to figure out exactly what she'd seen.

In due time, her mother came out to fetch her. "Dawn? Come inside, sweetie. It's dinner time."

Dawn turned around and raced back home as fast as she could, her bare feet pattering across the soft black sand.

"Mum! Mum! There was a boy in the water," she cried. "He was watching me play!"

Her mother just laughed, though, and patted her on the head. "Of course there was, dear. You can go play with your imaginary friend again tomorrow."

***

Curiosity was a cruel and irresistible mistress to any small child. Even though his mother had scolded him for slipping away without telling her where he was going, Cijal returned to the beach the next morning, just as the rosy glow of sunrise crept across the land from the east. He slipped into the tide pools and settled down to wait, anxious to see the little girl again, to watch her play in the sand – maybe even play with her, if she'd let him.

He'd dreamed about her the night before, about her pretty red hair and her green eyes. Although he was too young to understand the appeal of such traits, he was still fascinated by her. She was alien, but somehow familiar at the same time. He'd decided that he was no longer afraid of her – but the adult humans were a different story.

Shortly after the sun rose, his patience was rewarded. He saw a shadow appear on the dunes, which resolved itself into the little girl's outline. She paused and shot a furtive glance over her shoulder, then snuck on exaggerated tiptoes towards the water's edge.

Cijal hid himself amongst the tide pools, watching curiously to see what she'd do. This time, she came straight over to the pools, searching the early-morning gloom.

"Boy? Are you here?" she called softly. He didn't understand her language, but he knew from her body language that she was seeking him. It was the peak of high tide though, and the water level gave him excellent camouflage.

The boy tilted his head, considering. The choice was his. Would he let her see him or not? Right now, she couldn't see him even when she was looking right at him because his camouflage blended flawlessly with the water all around him. If he stayed where he was, she'd probably go away. If she went away, she might not come back. He decided that was an unacceptable risk.

Cijal lifted his head out of the water, deliberately breaking his camouflage. Only the top of his head broke the surface, just enough to show his grey-blue eyes, framed by a tangle of patchy white hair. Like his markings, his hair wouldn't begin to fill in properly until his early teens. Gentle waves lapped against the back of his neck and ruffled his hair, but he didn't move. He just waited, watching to see what she'd do.

The little girl jumped in surprise when she spotted him peeking at her above the surface of the ocean, then she put her hands on her hips and stomped her foot. "Come out here, boy!"

Cijal didn't understand the words but he knew what she meant. She was demanding he come out of the water and show himself, but her stance was a little too aggressive for his comfort. Suddenly wary, he crab-crawled sideways and hid behind a big, algae-covered boulder on the ocean side of the tide pools.

He heard the girl squeak as he darted away, and then he heard the sound of her footsteps splashing out into the water. The boy swam out a few meters and watched from amidst the breakers as she struggled to climb up onto the boulder, looking for him.

"Wait, come back," she called, reaching towards him. He darted away, fearful of being caught.

Just as he was about to flee back out to sea, he heard a heavy splash. He turned back, realising that the girl had slipped and fallen into the ocean. Concern sent a jolt of adrenaline through his little body. In school, he'd learned that the humans could not breathe in the water like his people, the Nereidis. He was amphibious, but the little girl was not.

She was thrashing in the water, frightened and out of her element. All the fear he'd felt moments before vanished, replaced by a different kind of terror. Now, he was afraid that the pretty little girl would die in the water and it would be his fault. Cijal couldn't bear that thought. He darted forward and caught her around the waist, dragging her back into the shallow tide pools so she could reach the land.

She hauled herself out the water and plopped down on the sand, coughing loudly and making pitiful, crying noises that he recognised as distress. Cijal couldn't tell whether the liquid running down her cheeks was tears or just salt water. It made him feel guilty to think that they might be tears. His people cried when they were sad or upset, too.

He sat down in the shallows and looked at her, wondering if her sounds would bring the adults again, but no one came. It must have been too early; like his parents, they were probably still asleep. His mother often complained that he woke too early in the mornings and that he should sleep later, like his older brother. Lauros was fifteen years old, and would soon be mature. Cijal had decided that the process of growing up must be very strenuous, since Lauros slept a great deal.

The little girl breathed deeply and coughed a bit more, until she cleared the last of the water from her lungs. He watched with concern, his head tilted to one side like a nervous puppy, uncertain what to do. Finally, she smiled and shoved her wet hair back out of her face, and then she said something he didn't understand. He just stared at her. The girl wrinkled up her face, repeated herself and jabbed a finger at him.

"I don't know what you're saying," he told her softly in his own tongue.

With an exasperated sound, the little girl pointed at herself and then held up five fingers. Suddenly, he understood. She was asking him how old he was. He nodded slowly, then pointed at himself and held up six fingers. She smiled broadly at him, an expression that lit up her whole face, and made his heart leap in his chest.

They spent the next hour learning to communicate, talking to one another with gestures and crude drawings in the sand. They spoke softly as they played, slowly learning words in one another's languages. She often called him 'boy'. He tried to explain that was not his name, but she didn't seem to understand. Every time he pointed to himself and said his name out loud, she would point to herself and then to the horizon. After a while, he gave up.

Still, she managed to explain to him that the little structure on the hill was her home, where she lived with her parents, people she called 'mummy' and 'daddy'. With great difficulty, she told him that they only lived there for a small part of the year, during the time when the water was warm and the sun shone most brightly.

She drew for him an elaborate picture in the sand, of herself and her parents going back to the big structures where they normally lived, followed by pictures of the moon. After a few minutes of confusion, understanding dawned: she stayed in the home on the beach for one month at the height of summer, then she went back to the other place.

Cijal was fascinated. He knew that many species of fish migrated to warmer waters when their normal feeding grounds got too cold, but he didn't know that humans did the same thing. He longed to tell his teacher, but if he told her then they'd find out he'd exposed himself to the land-walkers. His mother would be furious.

He cast a furtive glance back over his shoulder and sneakily probed for his mother's thoughts. She was still sleeping, but only just. He had to return soon, or he'd be caught.

The little girl looked at him, her head tilted at a curious angle. "Is your mummy waiting for you?"

Cijal didn't understand the entire sentence, but he identified the word that described a mother. With a solemn nod, he rose to his feet and pointed back at the ocean.

The little girl looked sad to see him leave. "Will you come back?"

He didn't understand the words specifically, but the context and her expression made her meaning clear. Cijal tilted his head and considered the question. Returning was risky, but it might be worth it. He decided that the potential for fun outweighed the risks, so he gave her a nod. The smile she gave him in return was so bright and joyful that it made his chest swell with pride.

With his decision made, the boy gave a universal wave of farewell, and vanished back into the ocean to return home.

***

Cijal returned to the beach often that summer, and usually found the girl waiting to play with him. He was always careful to stay on the part of the beach not visible from the house on the hill, so that her parents wouldn't see him, but they still managed to spend many hours together. They raced up and down the sand in gleeful abandon, chased small creatures together, built sandcastles in the shadow of the dunes when the heat of the sun grew overwhelming, learned about one another's cultures, and sometimes even fought – but it was all in fun.

When the morning came for her to return to the big structures, the little boy found himself feeling very sad. He'd gotten in trouble many times over the past month for sneaking out without telling his family where he was going, but he didn't mind that. What he did mind was that his playmate was going away for a very long time, and he was going to miss her. The girl seemed to sense his sadness, even though he didn't know the right words to express how he was feeling.

"I'll be back next year, I promise," she told him, then she knelt in the sand and drew the makeshift cartouches that they'd invented together, to reassure him that she'd return when the water was warm and the sun was high in the sky. That promise made him feel much better.

Then her mother called to her from the house. The girl called back. She hugged him quickly and scampered away. Just like that, she was gone from his life, and he was left feeling bereaved.

Every few days, the boy snuck back to the house to check, just in case she returned early, but she didn't. As the waters got colder with the coming of winter, he checked less and less; she'd been very clear that her family only stayed at the beach house when the water was warm.

Cijal's birthday came and went. He tried hard to forget about the little girl, but he couldn't. One morning, he realised that the water was not as cold as it had been the day before. Excited, he rushed to the house on the beach to check, but it was still too early in the season.

Every morning he checked for her, and every morning he went home disappointed. The little house was dark, empty, and quiet; there was no one there. He began to despair, and to convince himself that his brief encounter with the human had been nothing but a daydream. She wasn't going to come back. He'd never see her again.

Then, early one midsummer morning, his persistence was finally rewarded. When he snuck up to the beach and eased his head above water, he saw a light glowing in one of the windows of the beach house. His heart skipped a beat.

A few minutes later, the door opened and the little girl raced down onto the sand. She bounded along the beach until she was out of sight of her parents, and then stopped to search the shore for him with an expression that mirrored the anxious butterflies dancing in his belly.

He smiled to himself, marvelling at how much his friend had grown in one short year. Overwhelmed by the simple kind of joy that came from sharing life with a friend, he rose from his hiding spot and went to join her again.

***

Every year after that, the little girl returned at the height of summer and Cijal was waiting for her. Although he wished he could see her more often, he was content with the knowledge that she'd always come back to play with him, when the time was right.

One year, when he was ten years old, a terrible, squalling pink bundle came to the beach house along with the human family. The girl was eager to tell him about her new sister, but he wasn't sure what to make of it. The creature made horrible sounds that disturbed his sensitive hearing, all the way from the beach.

The girl was amused by his trepidation and teased him mercilessly, until her playful mockery made him laugh so hard that he forgot what he'd been worrying about. The noisy new baby turned out to be a blessing in disguise, because they were able to spend more time together as a result. Her parents were harried and distracted, and they often forget about their older child when she was out of sight.

Another summer ended. The waters went cold again. Another year passed, then another, as regular as the tides. His mother often questioned him about where he went after his classes, but as he got older she was less concerned for his safety. He told her that he was off playing with his friends, and she accepted the lie readily. But, in some ways, it wasn't a lie at all - he just neglected to tell her that his closest friend was a human.

The winter of his thirteenth birthday passed. Shortly after, he began to develop the first of his adult markings. Excited to show his friend, he waited anxiously for summer to come around again so he could share this new aspect of his life with her. Every day, he hurried to the house on the hill to wait for her, and every day he left disappointed. The waters got warmer and warmer until summer reached its peak, and then they began to cool again.

Cijal was left upset and confused. Every summer for the last six years, she'd arrived at that beach and they'd played together in the sun. This year, there had been no sign of her. Winter came and still he waited, watched, and checked for her every few days.

His fourteenth birthday came and went with no sign of her. The waters warmed again. A second summer arrived. With every passing day, anxiety gnawed at him more and more. She was his dearest friend. He trusted her. She wouldn't just leave him without saying goodbye. He worried that something had happened to her.

One day at the end of summer, there was a sudden flurry of activity in the house, but the human faces he saw were all strange to him. There was no sign of his friend's red hair, nor that of her mother or father. Cijal was disappointed and worried. She'd promised to come, but now she was gone.

He was fifteen years old, a young man well on his way to adulthood. Thoughts of his girl filled his every waking moment, but even the happy memories made his life miserable. Gradually, he grew more and more depressed. When his family tried to ask him what was bothering him, he just shook his head and said nothing.

As he grew older, hope faded farther and farther away – but it didn't disappear entirely. Every few days, he checked on the little house on the beach, but he only ever saw unfamiliar faces. Sometimes he roamed farther afield looking for any sign of her. He swam far to the north and south, but there was never anything to be found.

He worried that she was dead.

Still, he refused to give up hope. Hope was the only thing that kept him going. He was almost an adult now. He decided that when he came of age, he would go look for her. She was his friend and he owed her that much. He would do no less for any of his other friends, and she was so much more to him than that.

Another summer came.

The boy was nineteen years old.

Chapter 1

Dawn stared out of the window at the playing fields. It was the last day of school before exam leave began, and she couldn't focus on learning when the sun was shining so brightly and the sky was so blue. It didn't really matter, though. The teacher was no more interested in teaching than the class was in learning; in a few minutes, the senior year would be over, and they'd never see one another again.

As far as Dawn was concerned, graduation couldn't happen a moment too soon. Two days earlier, she'd finally turned eighteen and taken her first step into adulthood and independence. She finally had access to the inheritance her parents had left in a trust account for her, and while she didn't really care about the money it was her means to escape from life as a ward of the state.

Seven years earlier, a drunk driver behind the wheel of a truck had snatched away her entire family in a horrific, fiery crash. When she'd come out of the coma weeks later, her entire family was gone. Everyone, except Cijal.

She'd never had a chance to tell him what happened, and that upset her almost as much as losing her family. He was such a sweet boy, and she knew in her heart that her disappearance would have hurt him. Her thoughts drifted back to him, as they often did when she was alone. She wondered where he was, what he was doing – and how long he'd waited before he'd given up on her.

The bell rang, and so the stampede began. The majority of the students drained out of the classroom and into the hall in a dancing, cheering mob, leaving behind the few that wanted to say goodbye to their teacher. Dawn lingered for a moment to say her farewells, then she picked up her bag and headed out the door. As she walked, her mind drifted back to Cijal. He'd be nineteen now, she realised suddenly. Not a boy anymore. A young man.

She knew that she should go to university, but the idea of moving on with her life as if nothing had happened was just too painful. Every time she thought about the future, she ended up thinking about Cijal. She longed to talk to him again, even if it was just one last time. He was really the only aspect of her early life that was still a question mark. Everyone else was lost to her forever.

Dawn walked out into the car park and stared up at the vivid blue sky. The sun seemed far too bright for such sombre thoughts.

"Oi, sad sack. Where you been?"

Dawn glanced over and saw Jessica, her foster-sister and best friend, leaning against a wall. Jessica shoved herself away from the wall and sauntered over to give Dawn a casual shove. "I've been waiting around forever."

"Maybe you should have gone to class, then," Dawn answered dryly.

As much as she liked Jessica, they couldn't have been more different. Dawn was gentle and good-natured, never got in trouble, never broke the rules, and went out of her way to make a good impression on everyone she met. Jess, on the other hand, was a total ratbag, the epitome of the teenage rebel. She had tattoos and piercings, her dreadlocked hair was dyed black and fire-truck red, and she perpetually smelled of cigarettes. Dawn knew it was pretty much guaranteed Jess would get her in trouble one day, but she liked her anyway.

Jessica already had one of her smokes tucked behind her ear by the time she fell into step beside Dawn. The moment they left school grounds, Jess transferred the cigarette to her lips and pulled a lighter out of the pocket of her skirt.

"Jess, we're still in uniform," Dawn scolded her, scandalised by her friend's behaviour.

"So?" Jessica replied, laughing. "If they don't want us to make a bad impression on the community, then they shouldn't make us wear uniforms."

"You're so weird," Dawn told her.

"You say that like it's a new revelation," Jessica answered cheerfully. She took a dramatic pull of her cigarette, and blew a perfect smoke ring up into the sky. "So, what's wrong? You're moping. I always know when you're moping."

"It's just, you know, I don't know what I'm going to do now," Dawn admitted, shooting a plaintive look at her friend. "We're adults. We're supposed to do something. What do we do?"

"Well, I'm going to get a boyfriend, get pregnant, and chillax on the taxpayer's dollar while I learn guitar," Jess replied with a perfect deadpan expression. "Then, I'm going to make a band and get famous."

Dawn stared at her, uncertain whether or not she was being serious. Sometimes it was hard to tell. The silence dragged out until it started to get uncomfortable, and forced Dawn to say something.

"No, I mean, really."

"Oh, you mean *really*?" Jess echoed, and shot her a dark look. "How the hell should I know, Dee? No one expects me to amount to anything. My boss said I can start working full-time when I finish my exams, so I guess I'll do that." With a shrug, she flicked her cigarette onto the footpath and stomped on it. "But I think what you're really asking is what I think you should do, and you know I can't tell you that. You're the only one who can decide that for you."

"I don't even know, Jess," Dawn admitted, her shoulders slumping. "I don't even freaking know."

"'Fucking', girl. The word is 'fucking'." Jess grinned and pulled a package of gum out of her pocket. She peeled a stick, popped it in her mouth, and then offered a piece to Dawn. "Don't worry, I'll learn you to curse proper yet."

"No thanks," Dawn replied. "To both the gum and the swearing, by the way. I don't really want either. I'm having an existential crisis, here."

"Well, look," Jess said, turning serious – or at least as serious as she ever got. "We need to get out from under Mrs Farley's roof before she kills us, so I guess you have to get a job. We'll get a flat, maybe meet some guys, have some fun, and see where it goes from there. I can get you an application from work, but you'll have to hurry – the entry-level positions are going to fill up real fast after exams."

"Flipping burgers? Ugh, no way," Dawn groaned, shaking her head. Part of what Jess had said did strike a chord with her, though: specifically, the part about guys. Perhaps this was her opportunity to resolve the things from her childhood that still bothered her. "How about a change of scenery instead?"

"A road trip?" Jess laughed, snapping her gum. "My car's a piece of junk, Dee, but, if you wanna risk it..."

"We could go up north for a while," Dawn said, staring off into the middle distance as she pondered the idea. "I've got some money from my inheritance. I could paint; you could practice your guitar. We could just chill for a while. Plus, there's someone I want to look for..."

"Someone?" Jess echoed. "What kind of someone?"

"Just a friend from when I was a kid," Dawn replied, keeping her answer deliberately vague. There were some things she wasn't willing to tell anyone, not even her best friend. She'd made that mistake before, when she was a child. Her mother had laughed off her talk about the boy from the sea at first, but when she'd insisted a little too vehemently, she'd ended up having to see a child psychologist for six months.

She'd learned a very valuable lesson from that: don't talk about the boy from the sea. Ever.

"Hmm..." A thoughtful look passed over Jessica's face, then her expression brightened. "Hell, why not? We can do whatever we want within the bounds of decency and the law, right? Let's do it."

"After exams," Dawn said with a rueful smile.

Jess sighed heavily. "Fine, fine. After exams."

Chapter 2

"You haven't even told them you're leaving yet?" Dawn's voice rose almost to a shout. "Jess, you were supposed to hand in your resignation a week ago!"

"No way. My boss is a grade-A dickbag," Jess replied as they pulled into the car park of the fast food restaurant where she'd been working for the past two years. "I don't even mean a single dick in a bag, here, I mean like a whole giant, bulging sack full of dicks. Did I ever tell you about the time he tried to grope me, and then threatened to have me arrested for stealing if I told anyone? Yeah, that's the kind of dickbag he is. It took me all week to plan an appropriate revenge-signation … and to recruit a few helpers. I want it to be a surprise he'll never forget."

"Wait, wait, back up," Dawn gasped. "He groped you?!"

"Forget about that, I dealt with it," Jess replied. She slowly drove the car around to the back of the building and parked it across two loading zones. "Stay in the car, princess. I've got this covered. Watch and learn."

Jess stuck her head out the window and whistled sharply. A moment later, a couple of heads clad in black balaclavas popped up from behind an air conditioning duct on the roof of the building. One of the mystery men shot the girls a thumbs-up, and they ducked back down out of sight.

"You're not going to kill him, are you?" Dawn asked nervously. Even though she'd known Jessica for years, she still had a hard time anticipating her friend's actions and motivations. Jess had a tendency to act without thinking about the consequences, and sometimes Dawn thought that it was only sheer dumb luck that had kept her out of serious trouble. Problem was, now they were both old enough to be tried as adults.

"Don't worry, the only thing getting hurt here is that asshole's pride," Jess said cheerfully. She left the engine running and climbed out, sauntering up to the service door with over-exaggerated casualness. When she got there, she yanked the door open and yelled something through it that Dawn couldn't quite make out.

A few seconds later, a short, balding man in a crumpled business shirt stormed out. Even at a distance, Dawn could see that he was already red-faced and angry. She rolled down her window so that she could listen to the rest of the conversation.

"Where the hell have you been, Bentley?" the man yelled, jabbing a finger at Jess to punctuate his point. "You've missed three shifts! I've half a mind to fire you right now!"

"Well, sir," Jess replied, her voice so soft that Dawn could barely make out her words over the drone of the engine. "I have come to advise you of something very important."

Dawn glanced up and saw movement on the roof above their heads, but she couldn't see exactly what the masked men were doing.

"It better be really bloody important if you want to keep this job, girlie," he growled, stomping menacingly towards her. "I have a thousand other useless brats just waiting to fill your position."

Jess wasn't the kind of person that could be intimidated like that, though. She just laughed in his face, then she pulled a cigarette packet out of her pocket and very deliberately placed one cigarette behind her ear.

"Oh, it is terribly important, sir," Jessica replied in a fake British accent. "Most terribly so, indeed! I am here to tell you that – alas! – I am no longer in need of this most illustrious of employments, and that I must insist you immediately partake of delicious faecal matter and depart from the mortal coil. To put it colloquially—" She paused for half a second, then leapt back away from him and screamed at the top of her lungs, "Eat shit and die, motherfucker!"

Right on cue, the men on the roof sprang to their feet and upended buckets of chunky red fluid right over the unsuspecting manager's head, dousing him from head to toe. Then they cast their empty buckets aside, and grabbed more from out of Dawn's line of sight. She could hear their devilish whooping all the way from the car as they tipped those over the edge as well, coating the pint-sized businessman in tiny metallic sparkles and multi-coloured spots.

Jessica's former manager just stood there with his mouth open and his eyes wide, frozen in shock.

Jess cackled with glee as she darted away from him, sprinting back to the car. She threw open the driver's door and dove in, then put the car into gear and floored it. Dawn yelped in surprise as the rust-bucket leapt to life and tore out of the car park, leaving the stunned and filthy manager staring after them.

"What was all that stuff?" Dawn gasped.

"Jam," Jessica replied. Once the restaurant was out of sight, she eased off the accelerator and let the car fall back to a more reasonable speed. "Warm, extra-sticky jam, mixed with red food colouring. The other stuff was glitter and confetti mixed with cupcake sprinkles. He's not going to be forgetting that lesson any time soon, let me tell you!"

"Ew! That's horrible!" Dawn exclaimed, struggling not to laugh. It lasted about ten seconds before her willpower broke, and she muffled an unladylike giggle-snort with her hand. "Do you have any idea how long it's going to take to get that out of what's left of his hair?"

"Yes, yes I do." Jessica grinned wickedly, looking very pleased with herself. "He's going to be attracting flies for a week, I bet."

Dawn just groaned and slumped back in her seat. "Note to self: don't get on your bad side."

"Words to live by," Jess agreed. She sketched a salute, and then finally lit up her cigarette to celebrate her victory.

***

Their bags were all packed and waiting for them when they returned to the rambling old house they'd shared with the Farley family for the last few years of their childhood. Exams had finished a few days earlier, and both girls were anxious to get on with their adventure.

Mrs Farley was more than happy to see them leave. Now they were adults, she couldn't draw a wage from the government for their care and she didn't like any of them enough to feed them out of her own pocket. When they opened the door and went in to get their things, she just glared at them for a second, then pointedly ignored them. Mr Farley was nowhere to be seen, and the younger children were shrieking around upstairs, completely ignored and out of control like usual.

"Jessie!" a child's voice squealed from the landing. One of their foster sisters, a little girl named Charlotte, hurtled downstairs and threw herself at Jessica. "Jessie, Jessie, Jessie! Mitch is going to eat me - you have to save me!"

The boy in question, a youth of twelve, appeared at the head of the stairs with a sheepish look on his face. "Hey, I didn't say I was going to eat you."

"Yes, you did!" Charlotte cried, pointing an accusing finger at him. "You did, I heard you! You said you were going to eat my brains and make me a zombie!"

"Well, you don't have to worry about that anymore," Jessica cut in, interrupting the argument. "Mitch can't eat your brains if he's helping us carry our bags."

"Do you really have to go?" Charlotte's expression twisted, and suddenly it looked like she was going to cry. "If you go, who will protect me from the icky boys?"

"You'll just have to protect yourself. Those boys are wussies, you can handle them," Jess replied, patting the girl on the head. "We're too big to live here anymore, Charlie. We have to go be grownups now. One day, you will, too."

With some difficulty, she extracted herself from the child's grip and led the way up the stairs to the room she and Dawn had shared.

Their few belongings waited where they'd left them, packed into two backpacks, a suitcase and a couple of small boxes. It wasn't much, but it was everything they owned. Dawn had done most of the sorting and organising, of course; Jessica's idea of packing involved flinging things in random directions until something finally landed in the right place.

"But you'll come back and visit us, right?" Charlotte asked.

"I dunno, maybe," Jess said with a shrug. She picked up a box and planted it in Mitch's waiting hands, then looked at Charlotte. "We're going on an adventure, and we don't know what will happen. You'll just have to wait and see."

The girl thought about that for a second. Suddenly, she let out a squeal, leapt high in the air, and raced out of the room chanting, "Going on an adventure! Going on an adventure!"

The older kids watched her go, then exchanged looks and shrugs. Mitch mumbled something that Dawn couldn't make out, took his load of boxes, and left the room. Dawn and Jessica stood side by side for a moment, just looking at the room that had been home for so long.

"Good riddance," Jess said. She picked up her backpack, took the last box, and left. Dawn took one last look around, then she picked up her own backpack and the suitcase, and followed after the others.

She stopped in to say goodbye to Mrs Farley on her way outside. While their relationship couldn't really be called warm, it wasn't hostile either. They chatted for a minute, until it started getting awkward and Dawn sensed it was time to go. She hurried to the front door and down the walk, where Jessica's car was waiting for them.

Mitch had already vanished, and the other kids were nowhere to be found. Dawn glanced around, but she couldn't see any little faces peeking from the windows or staring out from amongst the bushes.

"They've already forgotten us," Jess commented.

"Looks like it," Dawn agreed.

They loaded their belongings into the trunk of the car, then bundled in and hit the road. It was going to be a long drive, in the heat of summer with no air conditioning, but Dawn didn't really mind. She was just excited to be on the move at last.

Once she'd made the decision to go, the wait had become excruciating. She'd spend the last few weeks fighting a nearly-overwhelming desire to ditch her exams and leave straight away. Sometimes, she found herself wondering if she was nuts, heading off on a wild goose chase to find some boy she'd known as a child. The whole thing sounded like a delusion, even inside her own head.

And yet, her memories of him were so vivid. When she closed her eyes, she could see his face. She remembered his eyes with a clarity that astounded her. He had been a quiet child, a little bit shy and sullen at times, but in her mind's eye she could still see the reflection of his soul mirrored in those storm-grey eyes.

She'd learned to read his emotions from the way he looked at her. Most of the time, he'd drifted between wariness and excitement, but as they'd grown older, she'd started to see a flicker of something else. The last time they waved goodbye, the look he'd given her had whispered of emotions so much deeper than mere friendship. At the age of eleven, she hadn't understood what it meant when a boy looked at her like that, but as she'd matured the pieces had started falling into place. Throughout her teenage years, she'd often found herself thinking of him, yearning to see him again but at a loss for where to begin. She even remembered a few of the words he'd taught her in his language. Most importantly, she remembered his name.

She smiled to herself as she thought back, remembering how bewildered he'd looked when she'd tried to explain to him that her name was Dawn. Dawn, like the sunrise. He hadn't understood. She wondered if he would be able to make sense of it now.

"What are you smiling at?"

Dawn glanced up and found Jessica watching her. She shrugged sheepishly. "I was just thinking how nice it'll be to see him again. My friend, I mean."

"Oh? Your mysterious childhood friend is a guy now?" Jessica's brows shot up. "You never said anything about chasing a guy."

"I said I was looking for a friend," Dawn protested, her cheeks flushing with embarrassment. "There's a fifty-fifty chance that friend might be male."

"Mm-hm. Mm-hm. And is he cute, this friend?" Jess lowered her eyebrows, and then waggled one suggestively. "I mean, if you're not into him and he's cute, send him my way."

"You told me like a month ago that you'd decided you were gay," Dawn reminded her.

"Yah, like I thought I was, so I went and watched the boys' swim team practicing just to be sure," Jessica replied with a shrug and a grin. "Turns out I'm not gay after all. I mean, I might be bi, I don't know. I'll figure it out one day."

"Whatever you say, Jess," Dawn replied. With a smile creeping across her face again, she put aside her irritation and sat back to enjoy the trip.

Chapter 3

Midday rolled around, and with it came the heat. Dawn sighed heavily and plucked the back of her t-shirt away from her sticky neck; even with the windows rolled down, she was sweltering. She grabbed a bottle of sunscreen out of her backpack and set about lathering on a fresh layer. Vulnerability to the sun was the redhead's curse, after all — even inside the car, she could still get fried.

"We're almost there, but we're going to need to stop for gas soon," Jessica said. Dawn glanced up and found Jess shooting pointed glances in her direction. She immediately understood that Jess was worried about the money. With petrol prices the way they were, she couldn't blame her.

"No worries," she replied. "I've got it covered."

"Thanks," Jess said, heaving a sigh of obvious relief. "We'll stop at the next petrol station and fill up."

Dawn nodded and resumed staring out the window. They were almost there. Then what? She didn't know where to start looking. As children, Cijal had always come to her, on the beach near the summer house. But the house was gone now, sold as part of her parents' estate, and even if she found the old house there was no guarantee Cijal would be nearby. Years had passed since her last visit. He must have given up on her by

29

now. Dawn bit her lip and blinked back tears as a sudden wave of despair hit her like a physical force, then she took a deep breath to steady herself. She had to try, and the old house was the only lead she had.

To her surprise, Jess didn't seem to notice her brief battle with her emotions. She glanced sideways and saw Jessica hunched over the wheel, staring down at the dashboard with an intense scowl.

"What's wrong?" Dawn asked.

"Man, I think the car's about to go," Jessica said. "She's making a really weird noise. You hear that?"

"I hear the car, but I don't know it well enough to work out if something's wrong," Dawn answered, concern rising in her gut. They were way out in the sticks, miles from the nearest town. She pulled out her cell phone and checked the reception. The signal weak and spotty.

"Man, I hope I'm wrong." Jessica made an inarticulate sound and patted the car's dashboard. "Keep going, baby girl. Just a little bit farther."

***

At that exact moment, Cijal was in a spot of bother of his own. Deep underwater, in the colony his people called home, he'd been on his way out of the door when his mother had waylaid him. Now, she stood blocking the doorway with her hands on her hips. Although she was easily a foot shorter than him, his mother still intimidated him. Adult or not, she would always be his mother.

"Just where do you think you're going, boy?" Nasara demanded, her expression set in a look of stubborn determination. It was a look that Cijal knew entirely too well, because it was the look she always got when there was a proverbial barnacle in her brassiere. "You know I arranged for that Jiras girl to pay you a visit this afternoon."

Cijal backed away, his posture turning defensive. "I told you, Mother. I'm not ready to pay court to anyone."

"Oh, yes you are!" Nasara stomped over and grabbed a handful of his necklaces, then she gave him a hard shake. "You're nineteen years old, Cijal. It's high time you started finding a mate. Just look how happy your brother is. And your father, for that matter!"

Cijal shot a pleading look at his father, but Eiran just held up his hands and gave him a shrug, as if to say 'sorry, kid. You're on your own.'

"Stop it, Mother!" he demanded, tugging his necklaces out of her grasp. Spurred by a jolt of anger, the kind of anger that only a family member could incite, he dodged around her and made a break for the door. "Just leave me alone! I will choose a mate when I'm good and ready! And as for my brother's happiness..." He stopped in the doorway and shot her a dark look. "Lauros is happy because being married gets him away from your incessant yelling!"

Nasara let out an indignant shriek and darted after him, but Cijal had inherited his father's reflexes as well as his size. He sprinted out the door and down the road towards the harbour, his bare feet thundering across the stone pavement. The colony had been built within the hollowed-out belly of a dormant volcano millennia before his birth, and it was lit and filled with air by technology that Cijal didn't fully understand. What he did understand was that the colony was not large enough to hide from his mother, and the open ocean offered him a respite the colony could not.

Cijal rounded a corner at top speed – and nearly bowled his brother over in the process. Lauros grunted in surprise and took a step back, using his superior body weight to keep his balance.

"Where are you off to in such a hurry, little brother?" Lauros asked, bracing his hands on Cijal's shoulders to help him get his balance back.

"Away from Mother, of course," Cijal replied, shooting a pointed glance back over his shoulder. He could still hear her in the distance, but she didn't seem to be getting any closer. A few people stopped and looked in the direction of the shouting, then shot knowing looks at the brothers. The colony was small enough that everyone, except for the odd traveller from elsewhere, knew about Nasara's infamous temper.

"Oh." Lauros' expression darkened. "I needed to go ask Father something. Should I wait until tomorrow, then?"

"Yes," Cijal said, with a grimace. "She's in one of her moods. I'd avoid her until she calms down, if I were you. I don't know how Father can put up with her when she gets like this."

"Ah, that's just what true love is, little brother," Lauros replied with a chuckle, clapping him on the shoulder. "It means loving someone forever, no matter how crazy they get."

"And she wonders why I'm not ready to start courting yet." Cijal rolled his eyes heavenwards, then looked at his brother again. "If you'll excuse me, I did actually have to be somewhere."

"Oh, of course." Lauros released him and stepped back with an affectionate smile. "I'll see you later, little brother."

"Later," Cijal agreed. With a wave of farewell, he

jogged off to the harbour and dove off the pier into the water.

***

Somehow, miraculously, the car survived long enough for them to reach the next petrol station. Both girls breathed a sigh of relief as they pulled into the tiny forecourt, but just as Jess was trying to manoeuvre the car around to the pumps, the engine spluttered and died.

Jess swore colourfully and tried the ignition again, but the only answer she got was an ominous clicking noise. They exchanged a look.

"Well, at least she got us this far, right?" Dawn pointed out.

"Whatever. I'm going to sell this bitch for scrap metal," Jessica snarled. She leapt out of the car and stormed over to the cashier's office; a few minutes later she was back with an elderly man in tow.

"I'm sorry, miss – I don't know how to fix a car," the old man spluttered, looking flustered and a little bewildered. "I'm happy to call a tow truck for y—"

"Aw, c'mon, you must know something. You're a guy, guys know cars," Jess whined, tugging at the man's sleeve. "Please, mister? We just need to get to town."

"I-I just operate the register," the man replied, looking helplessly back and forth between the two girls. "I haven't even owned a car in ten years."

"But I can't afford a tow truck!" Jess cried. Dawn heaved a sigh and went over to rescue them both.

"I can afford a tow," she said firmly, taking control of the situation away from her stressed friend. "Jess, you stay here and watch our stuff; I'll take care of this."

Dawn gently pried the cashier out of Jessica's grip and guided him back into the building. Once they were out of earshot, she smiled at him and said, "Sorry about her, sir. It's been a very long drive and we haven't eaten since breakfast."

"I really do wish I could help, but I don't even know how to change a tyre," the cashier answered meekly, pushing his spectacles up the bridge of his nose.

"It's all right," Dawn reassured him. "The tow truck will be just fine."

Once he was safely back behind his counter, the elderly cashier looked much happier. He fished out an old rotary-dial telephone and a phone book. While he was busy leafing through it looking for the right number, Dawn wandered around the pocket-sized convenience store. She decided that some sugar was in order to combat Jess' panic attack, so she picked out a couple of bottles of soft drink and a few chocolate bars. By the time she returned to the counter, the cashier was on the phone talking to someone.

He nodded a few times and made noises of agreement, then looked at her over his bifocals. "The gentleman at the garage in town says he'll tow you there for fifty dollars, then he can take a look at your engine and see if he can fix it. Would that be suitable?"

"That'll be perfect, thank you," Dawn replied. The old man nodded and spoke briefly into the phone to confirm the arrangement. After he'd finished his call, he rang up her food, took her money, and handed over her change. She stuffed it into her pocket and headed back out to where Jessica was waiting for her.

"Here, this will make you feel better," Dawn said, handing her one of the bottles of soft drink. "I got chocolate, too. You want the Snickers or the Picnic?"

"Ooo, my favourites." Jessica's eyes lit up at the sight of the naughty, sugary treats. She snatched one of the chocolate bars from Dawn's hand and calmed right down as she peeled off the wrapper. "Have I told you that you're my very bestest friend in the whole wide world?"

"Yes," Dawn replied, laughing. "You told me that the last time I bought you chocolate."

The two girls leaned against the car and waited for the tow truck. While they waited, Dawn made conversation about inconsequential things to keep her friend calm and distracted.

Half an hour later, the truck finally arrived. Soon, they were back on the road again, only this time they were bouncing along all squished together in the cab of the truck, with Jessica's poor little hatchback strapped firmly on the back.

Both girls were feeling a little wrung-out and fatigued, so they sat quietly and stared out the windows as the countryside rolled past. Occasionally, one of them would point out something interesting and the other would look, but that was about the extent of their conversation. They were too tired to do much else, and the noise of the truck made it hard to chat anyway.

It was well after lunch time when they finally arrived at the tiny township that had been Dawn's childhood home-away-from-home. She smiled to herself as they drove through the tiny block of shops that passed for the town centre; nothing had really changed at all, except that the one little café now advertised free Wi-Fi.

The garage was on the outskirts of town, near the road leading north-west to the beach. She'd driven that way so many times with her parents, past the tiny park filled with roses and the playground with the bright yellow slide. Suddenly she was surrounded by familiar landmarks, and the sight of them crushed the dark seeds of hopelessness that had been growing in the back of her mind.

The moment the truck came to a halt, Dawn sprang out feeling a renewed sense of purpose. She went to help Jess out of the cab, only to realise that her best friend had nodded off to sleep. Dawn laughed to herself, and went over to talk to the driver without disturbing her.

"Thanks for the ride," she said. "Do you know who we should talk to about getting the car fixed? We're new here."

"You talk to me, miss. I'm Bruce, the local mechanic," the man explained. He closed the driver's door quietly so as not to wake Jessica, then began unloading the hatchback with well-practiced efficiency.

"Oh, well that does make things easier," Dawn said, watching as he worked. "Do whatever you need to do to fix it, and I'll pay for it. Just... please, do us both a favour and don't tell Jessica what it costs."

"Yeah, I heard. She's a little high-strung," Bruce replied, chuckling good-naturedly. "I don't know about you, but I say we just leave her to sleep. We'll keep an eye on her if you want to pop next door and grab yourself a coffee. We'll call you when it's ready."

Dawn hesitated, glancing over her shoulder at the little strip of shops not so far away. "We have a few things in the car... it's not much, but it's everything we own."

"Folks around here don't steal from one another, lass," Bruce told her. "There are less than three hundred permanent residents here. Everyone knows everyone. Your friend and your belongings are as safe here as they would be in your own home."

"We don't have a home," she murmured without thinking. It took a few seconds before she realised what she'd said, and then she shot him a sheepish look. "I'm sorry, that sounded awful. We're orphans, and we just left our foster family. My family used to come here when I was a little kid, so we decided this was as good a place as any to make a fresh start."

"Ah," Bruce said, nodding his understanding.

"Don't worry, I have the money for the repairs," she hurried to reassure him. "From my inheritance. Jess gets a little panicky over money, though. I don't want her to freak out."

"It's fine, miss," Bruce replied. "Let's go get a few of your details down, then we'll get you sorted out." He beckoned for her to follow him, and led her into a tiny, air-conditioned office where a younger man, who introduced himself as Adam, the mechanic's apprentice and son, set her up with a small mountain of paperwork.

The two men chatted with her while she worked through the forms, then a few minutes later she was done and free to go. Dawn stood quietly in front of the door for a few minutes, just trying to organise her thoughts. She felt restless, anxious, and strangely out of sorts, though she had managed to put on a calm face for the mechanics.

Forcing her disquiet back down, she wandered over to check on her friend, and found Jessica still fast asleep. Her gut told her that Jessica would be safe there, so she decided to go poke around town a bit, to look for clues about where to begin her search.

Once she'd made the decision, she immediately felt better. The stores she passed on her way down the road weren't terribly helpful, though; the town was a tourist mecca that thrived on the seasonal trade brought by city people seeking peace for the summer, so most of the shops were either arts and crafts, souvenirs, or food. As she walked, she marvelled at how quiet the streets were for mid-December. The summer holidays were well underway and the town should have been teeming with life, but instead it was practically a ghost town.

A curious little store caught her eye, and she wandered over to peer in the window. The glare of the afternoon sun off the glass limited her vision, but what she could see was interesting. She pushed open the door and stepped in to the dark, stuffy interior.

Inside, she found an eclectic collection of everything from knitting wool to paints to musical instruments. In one corner, she spotted a couple of guitars on display beneath a faded neon sign advertising something she couldn't make out. Thinking of Jessica, she went over to look at them.

"Hi there!" a voice greeted her. Dawn jumped and glanced around, just in time to see a young woman appear from the back room. The woman waved to her, all friendly and full of smiles. "Sorry about the heat, the air conditioner's out. My name is Lily. Can I help you find anything? You look a little lost."

"Maybe," Dawn admitted. "I want to buy my best friend a guitar, but I don't know anything about them. Would any of these be good for a total newbie to learn on?"

"Oh, absolutely," Lily said. She rushed over and picked up the cheapest guitar, holding it up for Dawn to examine. "This one here. I recommend that your friend starts off with an acoustic like this before she moves up to one of the more expensive ones like an electric guitar, and this one is great value for money. It's durable, the strings are easy to replace if she breaks one, and it holds its tune wonderfully."

"You've used it?" Dawn asked, running her fingertips over the polished wood. Lily held it out to her and she took it, marvelling at how light it was considering its size.

"Oh yes," Lily replied, with a pleasant laugh. "I learned to play on it. It still sounds great even after all these years. Oh, and I offer lessons for a very reasonable rate, if your friend is interested."

"I think she will be," Dawn said. She handed the instrument back to the shopkeeper and gave her a shy smile. "I'd like to buy this one for her, but our car is getting fixed at the garage and I don't want to lug it around all day. Would you mind keeping it behind the counter for me for a couple of hours?"

"Of course," Lily agreed. "You come and pick it up whenever you're ready. We're open until five."

"I'll make sure to be back by then," Dawn said. She pulled her wallet out of her pocket and paid for the guitar, trading cash for a receipt. The storekeeper taped a copy of the docket to the guitar and tucked it behind the counter.

Dawn left feeling like she'd made a good investment. A few dollars for something that would make Jess so happy was worth every cent. Jessica had been talking about how much she wanted a guitar for as long as they'd known one another.

She resumed her directionless ambling and wandered farther into town, seeking inspiration or some clue as to where to begin. When she passed the café, she stopped briefly to pick up a sandwich and a bottle of water, but she didn't stay long. Restlessness kept her moving. She wasn't really looking for anything in particular, just some kind of idea about where to start her search.

When the revelation came, it came like a bolt from the blue and took her completely by surprise. One moment, she was just walking down the street with no goal in mind, and the next she was standing in front of a little real estate boutique, staring at a photograph of a building she would have known anywhere. There in the window was a sale notice for *her* beach house.

Dawn stared and stared, unable to drag her eyes away from the familiar outline. The building was nothing special, but it had been her home just as much as the place in the suburbs where she'd spent the rest of her childhood. No, the beach house had been more like home than the townhouse, because it was the one place on Earth where she'd been happiest. She found herself fixated, struggling to breathe, barely even blinking. In her mind's eye, she could see her mother calling her from the back porch, hear her voice, smell the salt on the breeze...

"Are you all right, dear?"

Dawn nearly jumped out of her skin. She glanced over and found a plump, middle-aged woman in a smart business suit watching her from the doorway with obvious concern.

"Uh... what?" Dawn stammered, struggling to assemble some semblance of coherent thought.

"Are you all right?" the woman repeated. "You've been standing out here for about five minutes, dear. And— are you crying?"

Was she crying? Dawn reached up to touch her cheek, and her fingers came away damp. She closed her eyes for a moment and drew a long, deep breath to steady herself, then summoned a pathetic attempt at a smile.

"Sorry, it's just, this house..." She trailed off, lifting a finger to delicately touch the photograph trapped on the other side of the glass.

"Ah yes, that's a lovely little house, right down by the beach, with stunning views over the ocean." The woman moved over to stand beside her, as though to comfort Dawn with conversation. "The current owners have put it up for sale because they can't afford the mortgage. Sadly, it's been on the market for a while now and it's just sitting empty. Economic downturn and all that."

Dawn swallowed hard, but the lump in her throat just wouldn't go away.

"I-I can't afford to buy it, but I would very much like to stay there. Do you think— do you think maybe the owners would consider renting it to me for a while? U-until they find buyers, that is?" she asked, fighting the nearly-overwhelming urge to cry. It was her home. Her home. The last time she'd seen that place, her family had still been alive. She wanted it so desperately, but her inheritance wasn't big enough to buy her a house.

"Well, I suppose I could ask," the woman replied, looking surprised. "But may I ask why? We have plenty of holiday rentals available – it's been a slow season so far."

"I don't want another one, I want that one," Dawn answered, ignoring how childish it sounded. She swallowed again and looked at the woman through eyes rimmed with tears. "Do you remember the last owners of that house? The Fitzpatricks?"

"Why yes, I do." The real estate agent sighed heavily and hung her head. "Oh, it was a terrible tragedy, just terrible. There was a car accident just outside of town. All of them died, except one of the girls I think. I never did find out if she pulled through."

Dawn struggled to form an answer but the lump in her throat felt like it was the size of a basketball and she couldn't make the sounds come out properly around it.

A few seconds later, she broke down completely and wept like the wound was still fresh.

Chapter 4

Cijal sat on the wet sand, staring up at the little house that had once been the home of the greatest joy in his life. Even though he'd never been inside it, he remembered the way happiness had flared up in his chest every time that door had opened, and she'd come out onto the porch. He usually avoided coming out of the water so close to the house, but no one had lived there in a very long time.

He probably could have gone up and looked through the window if he'd wanted to, but his instincts told him to keep his distance and just watch. Over the years, he'd come to respect the risk the land-walkers posed to his kind. Cijal was too young to have seen the destruction first-hand, but he'd studied all the stories about humanity in school: their massacres, the genocidal wars, the bombs that tore the sky to shreds and left poison in their wake. Humans could not be trusted. They were far too dangerous.

Not his girl, though. She would never hurt a soul, least of all him. He'd never been more certain of anything in his life.

The young Nereidis let out a long sigh and leaned back against his rock. It was low tide, so the tide pools were nearly empty and the sand was only slightly damp. Sometimes when he was feeling stressed or anxious, he liked to come up on the empty beach and sun himself. There, he could have peace and solitude, away from the burden of family and school. He'd gotten very good at leaving the colony stealthily over the years; no one knew where he went when he decided to vanish, and no one had managed to follow him. The beach – her beach, as he thought of it – was a place he could go to just sit quietly and think.

He'd never told anyone about his human, not even Lauros. No one would understand. The last thirty years had been good breeding seasons for the Nereidis; the summers had been warm, the winters mild, and food had been plentiful. There were many females around his own age for him to pick from, and more than a few had already expressed an interest in being his mate. It was not unheard of for a lonely Nereidis to choose a human companion in times of hardship, but he had no such excuse.

His people wouldn't understand, and they couldn't. It had taken years for him to understand his own feelings. The day he'd realised he was in love with that human girl had been the worst day of his life, because it was after he'd already lost her.

Without her, he felt so empty. Everything was useless. There was no point in doing anything, because she wasn't there to share it with him. The afternoon sun was so warm it made him uncomfortable, but he didn't want to leave. Perhaps if he just waited a little longer, then she'd come back and he could finally tell her how he felt.

"Who are you fooling?" he scolded himself. "She isn't going to come. She's gone."

Cijal's shoulders sagged. The dark cloud of depression descended over his thoughts, bringing him pain as surely as a knife to the heart. Sometimes he wondered if there was any point in going on. Without her, his life had no meaning.

He'd considered ending it just to get away from the pain, but his sense of honour forbade it. He still loved his family and his Nereidis friends too much to put them through that kind of grief, and if he did such a thing then he'd never know for sure what had happened to his girl. On the darker days, the only thing that kept him going was action. Activity distracted him from the terrible pangs of loneliness that burned in his heart and the back of his throat, and gave him the chance to fight back against the darkness that weighed so heavily upon him.

Cijal rose from the damp sand and returned to the ocean, to seek out something to distract himself. The ocean, the place where he belonged, and yet the last place he actually wanted to be.

***

It didn't take long for the real estate agent to put two and two together and figure out who Dawn was. When she did, she led the sobbing teenager inside and sat her down in the break room with a big box of tissues and a cut of hot tea.

Although she couldn't express it, Dawn was grateful for the woman's kindness. Nearly seven years had gone by since she'd lost her family, but at times the pain was just too much for her to bear. She'd been to see numerous grief counsellors, but no matter how many uplifting words she heard or kind faces she saw, it couldn't change the fact that her entire family was dead. Nothing would ever bring them back.

When the tears finally faded, they were replaced by emotional exhaustion. Dawn struggled to breathe and couldn't even work up the strength to thank the agent, whose name tag identified her as Marilyn Ascott. Every time she tried to say something, Marilyn just made soothing noises, patted her hand, and told her that she understood.

Eventually, Marilyn stood up and bustled out of the room. Dawn didn't know where she'd gone, but she was grateful to have a moment alone. Her hands shook uncontrollably, and she had to force herself to focus on drinking slowly to calm herself down.

Some days, the grief overwhelmed her. The counsellors had told her that the best way through it was to just let herself cry if she needed to, and often she did. She missed her family terribly. They'd been her entire world for more than eleven years. There was no one else; her grandparents were already dead, and she didn't know if she had any aunts, uncles, or cousins. If she did, she'd never met them.

Bleary-eyed and miserable, Dawn stared down into her teacup as if it might offer her some kind of relief from the pain. It didn't, of course. There was no solution for her, no magic wand that she could wave to bring her family back to life. No matter how hard she wished, they would sleep in their graves for all eternity, and nothing could ever change that.

Marilyn came to check on her, a worried look on her face. "I'm going to be a few minutes longer, dear. Will you be all right in here?"

Dawn looked up, startled. "I… yes, I think I'm okay. Sometimes, it just gets hard, you know?"

"I know, sweetheart. You just stay here and drink your tea, I shouldn't be too long," Marilyn replied in a soft, maternal tone, then she vanished back out the door and left Dawn alone again.

Twenty minutes later, the real estate agent returned with a few sheets of paper and a set of keys in her hands. Dawn had finished her tea by then and was staring into space, lost in her own thoughts. Her eyes only came back into focus when Marilyn sat down beside her.

"I'm sorry that took so long, dear," Marilyn apologised gently. "It took a bit of doing to get hold of the owners on such short notice. I managed to reach them though, and when I explained who you were they said that they're happy to let you stay in the house until they find a buyer, if you're willing to take care of it for them."

"I-I can do that," Dawn answered, tears of relief clouding her vision all over again. She rubbed her eyes impatiently to brush them away, and looked back at Marilyn. "What do we need to do? And how much would the rent be?"

"No rent, dear," Marilyn replied. "I told them who you are and what your relationship with that house is. All they want you to do is keep it tidy and maintained – mow that little lawn out the front, keep the house clean and organised, that kind of thing. You will need to pay the amenities, of course, but you can use the furniture in the house so long as you take care of it."

"Oh, yes, of course. That's so kind of them." Dawn sniffled and grabbed a tissue, sponging her eyes delicately. "I'm so sorry about this. I just... I came up here wanting to remember my childhood, but seeing the house again, it's just—"

"You don't have to explain, dear. I understand." Marilyn took her hand, squeezing it gently. "I didn't recognise you at first, but I do now. You were only a little girl the last time I saw you. The whole town was just devastated by what happened to your family. I'm glad to see that you survived, though. You've grown into such a beautiful young lady, your mother would be so proud."

"I hope so," Dawn replied. "I try to remember everything she taught me, just to keep her memory alive." She glanced up, and felt a twinge of guilt as she looked at the woman's kind face. "I'm sorry, I don't remember you."

"I would be surprised if you did, dear. You were very young." Marilyn soothed her anxiety with kindness, and then placed a few simple forms in front of her. "Here, I'll help you with these and then you can go get settled in."

They spent the next ten minutes filling in paperwork. Due to the unusual nature of the agreement, most of the forms had been drafted by Marilyn herself instead of being a standard legal form. Dawn didn't care about the particulars, she was too distracted; her emotions leapt back and forth between joy at the thought of seeing her old home again, and sadness at the idea of being there without her family.

At least Jess would be there. That would help. Her best friend would never let her mope for long, and it was hard to stay sad with her around. Once the paperwork was done, Marilyn gave her the keys and walked her to the street, where she hugged her and insisted that Dawn come and visit her family for dinner some time. Dawn agreed without hesitation.

As she walked back across town, she slid her hand into her pocket and felt the hard edges of Mrs Ascott's business card. She felt reassured by its presence, and happier for knowing that there was someone besides herself that remembered her family. Dawn decided that she would call her soon, and ask for more information about her parents. Her own memories were fractured and faded with age, and while Marilyn's probably would be as well, perhaps between the two of them they could reconstruct the pieces that were missing.

Dawn shaded her eyes against the midsummer sun, and suddenly realised that it was getting late in the day. She checked her watch and discovered that it was almost five o'clock – the afternoon had passed her by completely. The guitar was still waiting for her when she arrived back at the craft store, though Lily's smile faltered when she saw Dawn's face, still red and puffy from crying. Dawn just smiled back and avoided the subject completely.

By the time she left with the guitar, a second business card had joined the first in her pocket. This one was for guitar lessons, which Dawn decided she was going to buy for her best friend later on. In a small plastic bag, she carried a book Lily had recommended for learning the basics of guitar, and a few sheets of simple practice music.

The sun was still high in the sky when she left, but the footpaths that should have been teeming with summer tourists were conspicuously empty. Dawn shrugged it off and hurried back to the garage. Her first thought was to check on Jessica, so she went over to the tow truck and vaulted up to peer in the window.

The cab was empty.

Before she could panic, a muffled voice called her name. She turned and saw the mechanic's apprentice waving at her through the office window. A second later, Jess stuck her head up to the window and waved as well. She waved back and went over to meet them, the guitar awkwardly hidden behind her back.

"Hey, where have you been?" Jessica yelled. "We've been trying to call you for an hour!" Suddenly, she froze and stared intently at Dawn's face. "Why have you been crying?"

"I'll tell you later," Dawn replied. She fished her phone out of her pocket and laughed. "Well, that explains it. My phone is flat. I'm sorry. Here, I hope this makes it better." She grinned and thrust the guitar into her friend's hands. Jessica fumbled to grab it, her eyes widening in surprise.

"What? Whoa, where did you get this?" Jess cried, hugging the instrument to her chest. "Oh, man, I always wanted a guitar. Thanks, Dee. You're right, this totally makes up for it."

Dawn smiled, pleased to have brought her friend some kind of joy. "You're welcome. I appreciate you coming with me, so I figured I'd say thanks."

"Man, you know I'd follow you anywhere, sweets," Jessica answered, happily strumming her new guitar. "The car's done, by the way."

"Oh, of course," she said, shooting an embarrassed glance at Adam. "Sorry to keep you waiting."

"No worries, Jess kept me entertained," he replied. He handed her an invoice, careful to hide the figure from Jessica, and she handed him her debit card in return. The transaction only took a moment, and then Adam returned her card along with a receipt. He stepped out from behind the counter and led the two girls around to the back of the building, where their car was waiting.

Jessica climbed behind the wheel and Dawn took her place in the passenger seat. The moment they were belted up, Jess gave her a long, hard look. "So, why were you crying?"

"I found the old beach house my parents used to own," Dawn admitted. As briefly as possible to keep herself from bursting into tears again, she explained her encounter with Marilyn Ascott, and the arrangement she'd entered into with the current owners of the house.

When she finished her story, Jess leaned over and hugged her. "Aw, Dee. I hear you. But hey, at least we've got a place to stay, right? Fully-furnished and rent-free. Nice going."

"I guess." Dawn sighed heavily and looked down at her hands. "Let's just go. I'm really tired."

Jessica nodded and put the car into gear without another word.

Chapter 5

Shortly before sunrise the next morning, Dawn awoke feeling lost and confused. Although she'd slept deeply, her rest had been troubled by nightmares about dead family members and long-lost friends. In her dream she'd been running frantically, trying to find Cijal, but no matter how fast she ran he was always gone just before she got there. It took her a few minutes to figure out where she was: sleeping in a strange bed, in a familiar old house.

She pushed her anxiety dreams to the back of her mind as she rose and padded off to the bathroom. Dawn was a morning person by nature; Jessica, on the other hand, was a night owl. Given the choice, Jess would be up half the night and sleep all day. Dawn didn't mind at all, because that meant she had the mornings to herself. If she was going to find Cijal, she couldn't have Jess trailing along after her. As much as she loved her best friend, she didn't really trust her. There was a dark side to Jessica's nature that worried her at times. She'd only seen glimpses of it, but that was enough to make her a little wary.

A few minutes later, showered, dressed, and lathered with sunscreen, Dawn stood on the porch staring at the dark ocean. She was on the wrong coast to watch the sun rise over the sea, but the trade-off was that she got to watch the light of dawn creep up behind her, and set off a shimmering layer of sparkles along the crest of the waves.

She glanced over her shoulder and checked for any signs of Jessica, but there were none. Her friend was fast asleep in the master bedroom. Dawn had opted to sleep in her own room, even though it was smaller. All the furniture was different, but the room itself was familiar and comfortable.

Content that she was alone, Dawn picked her way down the steps and onto the sandy beach grass beyond. She went carefully at first, watching for broken glass and any other sharp-edged trash, but the beach was tidy and surprisingly litter-free.

The black iron sand sparkled underfoot as she climbed the low dune directly in front of the house and then half-walked, half-slid down the far side onto the beach itself.

A pang of nerves twisted her gut as she walked down to the water's edge and stood there, letting the gentle waves caress her toes. She looked down at them thoughtfully, then swept her foot through the shallow water, sending a sheet of sparkling droplets through the air. She lifted her head and looked out across the water, studying the distant waves.

How would she tell him she was there? As children, their communication had been rudimentary at best. She didn't know how to contact him, he'd always just... been there. Anxiety twisting her stomach to the point of nausea, she stared up and down the beach in search of some kind of inspiration, but found nothing. She simply didn't know enough about him. Hell, she didn't even know what he actually was.

A hundred metres down the beach, she spotted a familiar boulder out amongst the tide pools. That seemed like as good a place to start as any, so she hurried down the beach, her footsteps raising a cloud of loose sand in the shallow water.

A tiny crab fled from her path and she paused to watch it run, thinking of all the times that she and Cijal had chased the little creatures together. The memory brought a smile to her face. Cijal had been much better at catching them than she was, and she'd always been so jealous of his athleticism. Every so often, he'd taken pity on her and cornered one for her to catch, just to keep her interested in the game.

"Who are you now, Cijal?" Dawn wondered aloud, her gaze drifting back to the horizon. "What do you look like? Are you much taller than me? Has your hair grown out? Would I even recognise you if I saw you?"

She sighed softly to herself, picking her way between the smaller rocks lining the tide pools until she finally reached the huge boulder. With great care, she climbed up onto the ring of smaller boulders that surrounded it, and used them to reach the top of the big one. It was wet and slippery with algae, but she'd deliberately worn her oldest, rattiest clothing so that she wouldn't have to worry if it got ruined. Dawn settled on top of her boulder, drew her knees up against her chest, and stared out to sea.

"Cijal?" she called softly.

There was no answer, but that didn't surprise her. The ocean was a big place. Still, she felt the need to try.

"Cijal, I'm sorry I was gone so long. Please come back," she whispered to the impassive ocean, and then she closed her eyes and waited.

An hour passed, and then another. Cijal didn't come.

***

"Are you paying attention, Cijal?"

Cijal snapped out of his daze at the sound of his teacher calling his name. For a moment, he'd been a million miles away, or perhaps just a few. Sometimes it felt like someone was thinking about him, and he wondered if it was his girl. His people were naturally telepathic — that was how they communicated underwater — and the ability was much more sensitive between people who shared an emotional bond.

"I apologise, Magister," Cijal said. He sketched a quick bow and turned his attention back to his lessons.

The grizzled old warrior grunted and pointed to one of the other cadets in his training group. "Square off with Sarok. Bare fists. If you think you can sleep through my class, then I want to see how much you've managed to learn by osmosis."

"Yes, sir." Cijal bowed again, and went over to his classmate as instructed.

The two young men stepped into the combatant's ring together. Sarok extended a closed fist to him, as tradition demanded. Cijal's response was equally traditional; he lightly tapped his knuckles against Sarok's, then dropped down into a fighter's crouch.

The Magister shouted a command, and the two youths went to war.

***

Sometime around midday, Jessica came looking for her. Dawn lifted her head when she heard her friend's voice calling her from the top of the dunes. She'd been sitting there so long that her joints were stiff and her clothing was soaking wet from sea spray.

While she'd been lost in thought, the tide had snuck in. She wasn't worried, though. The water was no more than waist deep on her now that she was older, and reefs farther out to sea kept the waves gentle. Careful of the rocks concealed beneath the surface, she slid down from her perch and waded back to shore. Jessica met her at the water's edge with a quizzical look on her face.

"Have you been out here all morning? What are you doing?" she asked.

"Just thinking," Dawn replied. "Watching the ocean helps me relax." She gave her friend a wistful smile and headed back towards the house, with Jess trailing behind her.

She'd decided that the only solution to her dilemma was to wait and be patient. If he still remembered her, then eventually he'd come to her. That was the big question, though: Would he remember her? Would he care enough to come looking for her after all these years? Cijal had been her most loyal friend, but that was a third of a lifetime ago. Things changed over time and logic said that he would have given up on her by now, but her feelings certainly weren't logical so maybe his weren't either.

"We should go get some groceries," Jess said. "There isn't much in these cupboards. I went out this morning and scoped the town, pretty sure I know where we can shop."

"You're right," Dawn agreed, though her head was elsewhere.

"I can go if you want to stay here," Jessica suggested, shooting Dawn a look. "You don't look so good. Are you feeling okay?"

"I'm fine," she said. "It's just that this place has a lot of memories. This was the last place I saw Mum and Dad alive, you know? It's like I can feel their ghosts watching me."

The lie came easily, a little too easily, because it was based on the truth. Even when she was focused on Cijal, her family was never far from her mind. In her heart, the two were intrinsically linked, even though they'd never met one another. He was family, too, but in a different way.

"Maybe it wasn't such a good idea to come here," Jess said, grabbing her arm. She turned Dawn to face her and looked her straight in the eye. "Are you sure you're going to be okay?"

"Yes, I'm sure," Dawn replied, then she smiled and hugged Jess. "I need this. I need closure. This is like therapy for me, you know? It's going to take me some time to relax, but I need a chance to say goodbye before I can move on. I never had that chance."

"I hear you," Jess said, hugging her back. "I never had that problem with my parents, but I get it. I had plenty of time to say goodbye to Mum before the cancer got her, and when Dad killed himself, he literally said it. At least both of my parents had the chance to tell me they loved me one last time. I'm not sure how I'd cope without that."

"Well, this is a depressing conversation," Dawn said. She shoved Jess away and gave her a playful punch on the arm, then smiled at her. "Come on, let's go get some groceries."

Their decision made, the two young friends linked arms and went off about the important business of filling their fridge, and their bellies.

***

Two hours later, their fridge was full of food, some of it healthy but most of it not. Dawn stood at the stove scrambling eggs, while Jess sat at the tiny kitchen table strumming her guitar tunelessly. Dawn barely even noticed Jessica's troubled attempts to learn her instrument; she was too busy dividing her attention between cooking and staring out the window at the ocean.

"Fark, I suck at this," Jessica groaned. "I think I do need those lessons after all."

"I thought you might." Dawn grinned and waved a spatula in her general direction. "I told you, I'll even pay for them for you."

"I know, but your inheritance won't last forever," Jess protested. "A few months ago, you were just as broke as me."

"It's just for a little while, until you find another job." Dawn turned her attention back to the stove as she dished up their lunch, dividing the eggs between two plates. It was a little late in the day for breakfast food, but it was a simple meal that they both enjoyed, which was good enough for her. "Speaking of jobs - did you have any luck this morning?"

"Yes, actually," Jessica said, her expression suddenly brightening. "Adam said his mum's work is looking for a go-fer. It's not much, just making coffee, doing the filing, and answering the phone a few hours a week, but it pays okay. He said he'd put in a word for me."

"Hey, that sounds perfect," Dawn replied. She picked up the plates, carried them over to the table, and sat down. "You know, I think that guy likes you."

"I know he likes me," Jess said coyly, "since he asked me out yesterday while we were waiting for you."

"Oh, really now? What did you say?" Dawn asked, secretly delighted. A boyfriend was just what she needed to distract her best friend while she was hunting for Cijal.

"Well, let's see. He's nineteen, cute, has a good job, and can fix a car. What do you *think* I said?" Jess grinned and wiggled an eyebrow suggestively. "I said 'hell, yes!' His family is organising a big barbeque tomorrow night, and he wants me to be his date. It's a community event, so you're invited too."

"Well, that does sound nice," Dawn said thoughtfully, her smile fading a little bit. "Some of these people knew my parents. Mrs Ascott did. I wonder..."

"It can't hurt to ask, sweets." Jess reached over to pat her arm sympathetically, and then grabbed her place and started shovelling down her food. Dawn did the same, but she couldn't help worrying that finding out more about her long-lost family was going to be even more painful than losing them in the first place.

Chapter 6

"What on earth are you wearing?" Dawn asked, laughing merrily at the sight of her best friend all dolled up for her date. "Seriously? You're wearing a dress? You hate dresses, Jess. Who are you and what have you done with my BFF?"

"Shut up," Jessica whined. "I just want to look nice." Suddenly, she rounded on Dawn with a look of horror on her face. "Do I really look silly? I don't want to look silly."

"You don't look silly, it just… surprised me," Dawn replied, struggling to suppress her fit of giggles. "I've never seen you in a dress, and after all the complaining you did about having to wear a skirt to school, I never imagined you'd put one on willingly." She looked her friend up and down, then clicked her tongue disapprovingly and pointed at her feet. "Jess, you can't wear steel-cap boots with a floral-print dress. Go put some cute ballet flats on."

"I don't have any ballet flats," Jess said, staring down at her feet as though afraid they were going to bite her. "These are the only shoes I've got, except for my old school shoes."

"I have a pair that will go with your outfit," Dawn replied. "They might be a little big, but they'll do. Go take those boots off while I find them."

Dawn shooed Jess away, and went off to find the shoes, which didn't take long since neither of them owned a great deal of anything. The shoes were nothing fancy, but they didn't need to be for a casual back yard get-together. Dawn had opted for a simple pair of denim shorts, a t-shirt, and running shoes – but she wasn't there trying to impress a boy. Struggling to hide her amusement, she took the flats to Jessica and helped her friend put her dreadlocks up into a cute ponytail. Once the transformation was complete, they stood in front of the mirror examining the effect.

"Congratulations, Jess," Dawn teased. "You almost look like a normal person."

"Is that a good thing?" Jessica asked, looking just about as worried as Dawn had ever seen her.

"Yes," Dawn reassured her. "Go start the car; I'll meet you out there in a second."

She patted Jess on the shoulder one last time and went off to the kitchen to fetch the salad she'd prepared as their contribution to the evening's festivities. While she was there, she glanced at the sea shore – then she did a double-take. For a second, she thought she'd seen movement out there, but the glare of the afternoon sun on the horizon made it hard to tell.

By the time she'd shaded her eyes, there was nothing to be seen. Disappointment left a bitter taste in her mouth, like ash on the back of her tongue, but she forced herself to hide her frown and hurried out to the car.

***

Cijal stared at the house on the beach, his heart thundering so loudly that he felt certain that it would break his camouflage. There had been movement in the house, and for a second he'd seen a ghostly-pale face in

62

the window. He was too far away to recognise the face, but as the human turned away from the window, he thought he'd seen a flash of red hair. The angle of the sun made it hard to be certain, but he thought maybe, just maybe, it might have been her...

There was no way for him to be certain. The human was gone, and he heard the rumble of one of their smelly vehicles leaving the house. With a mixture of excitement and trepidation warring inside him, he settled down in the tide pools to watch, and to wait.

He waited for hours, until hope began to fade away again. Perhaps he'd imagined it, or it was just another stranger in her house. As the hours wore on, hope turned to anxiety, and anxiety turned to despair. The afternoon sun was hot, and it made him uncomfortable. Eventually, the discomfort started to turn to pain, but he didn't want to leave until he was certain.

Shortly before dusk, when the shadows were starting to get longer and cast the world into stark relief, he heard the faint whisper in the back of his mind that told him his father was calling to him. It was time to come home. The waters were dangerous at night. Dark things rose from the deep, and a lone Nereidis was easy prey.

Reluctantly, he drew away from the beach and slid beneath the waves, then swam back to the colony where his family waited for him.

***

The barbeque was a friendly affair that attracted most of the local community, yet despite the kindness of the people all around her, Dawn eventually ended up feeling out of place. No one was cruel or judgemental – quite the opposite, in fact. They were a little bit *too* nice, and it left her wondering if news of exactly who she was had already spread through the community. Marilyn did seem like the chatty sort.

In search of a few moments of solitude amongst the throngs of half-familiar faces, she took her paper plate full of egg salad and sausages and wandered down towards the beach. She sat down cross-legged right on the edge, where the grass met the sand, and picked at her food half-heartedly.

She could hear the voices of all the people on the White family's back lawn having a merry old time, and yet somehow the sound made her feel sad. They would welcome her with open arms if she let them but she wasn't sure if she was ready to accept it yet. Dawn heaved a sigh and took a sip of her lemonade.

She'd told people that she'd just returned in search of her family, but the ease with which the lies came off her tongue disturbed her a little bit. It wasn't in her nature to lie, and having to do so made her feel as if she was living in purgatory, trapped between worlds with no way to move forward or backward until it was time. Even with friends all around her, she felt lonely. He was the one part of her life that had been reliable and permanent. She needed him, desperately. After waiting so long for the freedom to be able to go seek him out, waiting a few more days – or even a few more hours – was agony.

Thinking about him took her appetite away. She set her plate aside and drew her legs up to her chest, wrapping her arms around them. The heat of the day still lingered, and yet she felt cold inside.

"I thought I saw you going this way," a gentle voice said behind her, interrupting her thoughts. Dawn looked back and saw Marilyn Ascott making her way towards her. "What are you doing out here all by yourself, sweetie?"

"Just thinking," she replied. Another lie that was starting to come just a little too easily, her canned excuse whenever someone caught her staring wistfully out to sea. How else could she explain what she was doing, or who she was waiting for? No one would understand. They couldn't. They'd think she was crazy.

"Well, come back to the party, dear," Mrs Ascott said, smiling kindly. "I found some photographs I wanted to show you while I was going through one of my old albums."

Despite her emotional exhaustion, Dawn found herself nodding obediently. She rose to her feet and allowed herself to be led back to the festivities, even though her heart lingered beneath the distant waves.

***

Later that evening, when the eating was over and the drinking was about to begin, Dawn slipped away and went home. She couldn't find Jessica anywhere, but it was only a few kilometres back to their house and the evening was clear and warm, so she decided to walk.

Her feet crunched softly over the gravel driveway as she set off, her hands tucked comfortably into her pockets. At the last moment, she veered off the driveway and down a low bank onto the beach. The sound of her footsteps changed timbre as the gravel beneath her gave way to firmly-packed sand.

She could have walked along the road, but the beach ran parallel and she was probably safer with the crabs and the sleeping seagulls than on the road with the drunken drivers. There were no street lamps, but the stars were out and the moon was almost full; between the two of them, they lit up the world almost as bright as day. Plus, on the beach there was a chance, however slim, that she might be spotted by the one person she actually wanted to see.

As she made her way toward home, she ran her fingers thoughtfully around the edge of the photograph in her pocket. It was an old Polaroid, taken when she was about six or seven. Her parents looked so young and happy, and the love in their eyes... she could feel it radiating off them, even across the bridge of time. She owned a few other pictures of her parents and sister, but every one of them was precious to her, a little glimpse of a memory that could never be reality again. Of course, there was one member of her family missing from every photograph. The only image she had of him was the one in her head.

Tiny waves whispered softly against the shore as she walked, rimmed with foam, pussy-footing their way in from the deep ocean beyond. She glanced at them every so often, wondering what it was like to live out there in the bottomless depths. She'd never been able to ask. Her imagination found many possible answers to her question, but the only way to know for sure would be to ask him.

She wondered if he was cold, wherever he was. Would creatures like him feel the cold? The water was warm at this time of year, but that was near the surface. How deep did the sun's rays penetrate? There were so many questions left unanswered. What did he eat? What did he wear? What did he do for fun? Perhaps now that they were adults she'd be able to communicate with him properly, and finally find real answers to her questions.

The only problem was that she had to find him first.

It took her about half an hour to reach her house. She climbed the familiar dunes and went up the back stairs onto the porch, fumbling in her pocket for her key. The house was dark and empty, with no sign of Jessica at all.

Dawn pulled out her phone and checked for messages, but found nothing. She shrugged it off, and decided that it must have been a very good date indeed. Unless told otherwise, she would assume the house was hers for the night. So, she did what any healthy eighteen-year-old would do: she locked the doors, and put herself to bed.

***

Cijal lay awake, staring at the carved stone ceiling above his bed. Every time he closed his eyes and tried to sleep, he heard a voice calling his name. Each time, he came awake and tried to listen to see who or what it was, but the voice vanished without a trace.

There was a strange hollowness inside him, an emptiness that was neither loneliness nor despair. It was something else. It took many hours for him to full understand what it was: anticipation. A part of him was trying to say something, but he couldn't figure out what.

Whatever it was, he knew that he would have to go back to that beach the following afternoon, once his classes were over and he was free to do as he liked. He would keep going back until he had an answer. One way or another, he had to know for sure.

Sleep was a long time coming that night.

Chapter 7

Time practically stood still at their little beachside retreat. A week passed, but it felt like an eternity. Jessica was often out and about, either at her new job or spending time with Adam, while Dawn found herself becoming more and more of a home-body. While Jess was gone, Dawn spent her mornings down on the beach, staring out to sea, and her afternoons at home, cleaning, painting or reading.

After a few days of boredom, she started bringing things down to the beach with her, so that she'd have something to do while she waited. At first she'd chosen simple things, like a book or a sketch pad. Today, she decided she was going to paint. If Cijal was going to keep her waiting forever, then she may as well use the time productively.

Dawn set her little easel up in the sand and placed a blank canvas on it. As she mixed up her colours and organised her brushes, she found herself feeling strangely happy despite the incessant ghost of loneliness. She loved to paint, and it was the one thing she really had a talent for. Although she doubted that she would ever be able to make a living from it, it gave her a means of self-expression and helped her feel good about herself.

The sun gradually rose higher in the sky as she worked, but her big beach umbrella protected her.

Slowly, her painting began to take shape as she worked with her brush, adding a touch of blue here, a little green there. Although she preferred portraiture, there was something very peaceful about painting a landscape. She'd chosen to paint the sea because it was beautiful, and it seemed like a logical choice since it was right there in front of her. She didn't really need to look at it to render its likeness, but she did occasionally glance up just to check that she was capturing it accurately.

She lost track of the time as the hours rolled by. The shadow of her umbrella shifted slowly, but she paid no attention and let herself get wrapped up in her work. Normally she went inside just before midday, but not today. Lunchtime came and went, and still she painted on.

Then, suddenly, something changed between one glance and the next.

She barely registered it at first, but a few seconds later she realised that she could see the faintest distortion out in the waves, barely more than a shimmer. It was the kind of distortion that a person wouldn't even notice unless they'd seen it before. Most people would dismiss such a thing as a trick of the light, but Dawn knew better. She stared hard, shading her eyes with her hand.

When realisation finally struck home about what she was seeing, it hit her like a sledgehammer. She dropped her paintbrush, leapt to her feet, and raced down to the water's edge. She'd seen that kind of distortion before, when Cijal had been hiding from her or her parents. She had no idea how he did it, but in her heart she knew it could only be him. She just knew it. It *had* to be.

"Cijal!" she cried, throwing caution to the wind. "Cijal!"

Dawn raced the last few meters across the beach and splashed out into the water, her feet sending showers of sparkling droplets up with total disregard for stealth or the state of her clothing. She didn't care, she couldn't care. Praying that he would see her, she waded out to waist deep, frantically waving her arms in hopes of attracting his attention.

There was no response of any kind. The distortion just vanished, as suddenly as it had appeared.

Heartbroken, she waded out of the water and plopped down on the wet sand just beyond the tide mark, fighting the urge to cry. A few tears escaped before she could stop them, but she didn't bother to wipe them away. There was no point. She was all alone. She'd be alone forever. Everything she'd hoped for was just an illusion, the made-up world of a little girl that had no basis in reality.

Dawn buried her face in her hands and surrendered to her tears. She was so distracted that she didn't hear the sound of a streamlined body breaking the surface of the water, the tread of feet upon the sand, nor the drip of water from skin. She heard nothing... until he spoke.

"I didn't realise you knew my name."

The voice was deep and powerful, nothing like the childish trill she remembered from her youth. Dawn's head jerked up, and she stared in wide-eyed shock at the man standing before her. He was no longer a boy in any sense of the word; now, he stood tall and powerful, his muscular body outfitted in close-fitting garments that looked more like skin than cloth.

His white hair had grown out thick and full and now reached past his shoulder blades, but it was his complexion that had changed the most. As a child, his skin had been a soft grey, like a dolphin. As an adult, it had taken on a more bluish cast, and was adorned by exquisite, multi-coloured markings. Shades of gold and pink, purple and green wove across his skin, adorned his temples and the sides of his neck, and wound over his broad shoulders, chest, and all the way down his arms. They were beautiful, intricate, and delicate, completely alien to anything she'd ever seen before.

"Cijal?" she whispered, struggling to make sense of what she saw. The difference between a boy of twelve and a man of nineteen seemed impossible.

He nodded once, watching her with uncertainty written on his face. She couldn't blame him; the changes he saw in her must have been just as much of a shock.

But that didn't matter, she realised suddenly. It didn't matter at all. What mattered was that she'd found him. He was alive, real, and right there in front of her. Emotion and adrenaline surged through her, forcing her upright before she quite knew what she was doing. Her feet splashed through the shallows again as she rushed out to him and threw her arms around his neck. She half expected him to vanish into thin air, flee, or even fling her away, but he didn't. He caught her and held her close against him, hugging her just the way a human would. Whatever he was, she didn't care – he was there and he was definitely real.

"You left me..." His words were soft but clear, whispered right beside her ear. Even without seeing his face, she could feel the pain behind them. She eased herself back and looked up at him, her vision blurred by tears.

"I didn't mean to. I didn't want to," she struggled to explain, battling down the terrible pain that came when she thought of the death of her family. "I'm so sorry.

There was... an accident. My family died, and I was badly injured. When I was well again, the state gave me to another family to be raised. I came as soon as I could."

As she explained, she saw the pain in his eyes fade away, only to be replaced by a different kind of agony: the sadness of sympathy for a friend.

"I feared something might have happened to you," he said, his voice hardly more than a murmur. "But I feared more that you might have simply forgotten about me."

"Never," she answered, hugging him fiercely, pressing her face up against his smooth skin. His skin had a strange texture to it that felt very different to hugging another human, but it was not unpleasant. It was not slimy or moist in any way, but firm, taut, and pleasantly warm. Even though he'd been underwater just moments before, the moisture had already rolled off and left him almost completely dry.

Suddenly, another realisation struck her. She jerked back and stared at him in confusion. "Wait – you speak English now?"

"Yes," he replied, his smile wry and a little bit sheepish. "When I finished my general schooling, I decided to become a Watcher. They teach us several human languages as part of our vocational training. I hoped that if I found you again, being able to speak your language would help."

"You were looking for me?" she asked softly.

He swallowed hard and looked down at her, his smile changing to one of fragile honesty. "I never stopped looking for you."

Unable to contain her emotions any longer, Dawn pressed her face up against his broad chest and wept unabashedly for what felt like a very long time. He just stood there and held her while she cried, strong, silent, and understanding. When she finally calmed down again, she gave him a shy smile.

"You got so tall," she said.

"I grew up – as did you, I see," he replied, his voice heavy with emotion. He lifted a hand and touched her chin gently, almost reverently. "It brightens my heart to see you alive and well. I have missed you."

"I missed you, too," she admitted without hesitation. A sudden spike of mixed emotion jolted through her, and made her want to laugh and cry all at the same time. "I can't believe it. Come on, let's get you out of the sun, I know you don't like it. We've got so much to talk about!"

Dawn grabbed his hand and half-led, half-dragged him up the beach to the shadow of her umbrella. They sat down side by side, and for a moment there was silence.

"I'm sorry to hear about your family," he said eventually, touching her hand tenderly. "I know that you loved them very much."

Dawn sighed and nodded. "I still love them – I'll always love them. But finding you is like getting a little piece of them back. It's a bit silly, but I was starting to wonder if you were a figment of my imagination."

"I understand," Cijal admitted. "Sometimes I felt the same way. My friends think I am very peculiar."

"Your friends know about me?" she asked, absently reaching up to touch a strand of his hair. As a child, his hair had always been short and patchy, like a biological afterthought. Now it was thick and lustrous, not quite truly white but almost iridescent, like mother-of-pearl.

"No. I tell them I like to go look at the reefs by myself. That's why they think I'm peculiar." His smile faded away and his gaze dropped down to the sand. "If they knew I was searching for a human girl, then... I do not know what they would do. They would not be happy."

"Your people don't like humans?" she asked.

He glanced at her and shrugged, a familiar, strangely human gesture. "Few land-walkers know of our existence. There are some... groups that we occasionally trade with, but our elders feel it's safer to keep ourselves hidden from the rest. Our technology is significantly more advanced than yours, and you know as well as I how ruthless some can be when they see an advantage to be gained." He looked down at her hands, gently turning her delicate digits within his grasp as though studying them. "I agree with the decision of the elders to keep us hidden, but you... you are different."

"I understand." Dawn frowned to herself as she thought it over, and then sighed. "I grew up knowing about you, so I've always just accepted that you're there, you're my friend, and that's all that matters. But a lot of humans are... not very nice."

"I know," Cijal replied. "We were human once, too. Our bodies are different now, but we still share the same basic nature."

Dawn's head jerked up, to stare at him in wide-eyed shock. "You're human? But... how?"

"We *were* human, thousands of years ago," he corrected her. "At least, that's what our historians teach us. I don't know the exact details, but there was some kind of technological discovery that transformed us into what you see before you." He held out his hands, gesturing to the obvious differences between them. "The legends vary depending on who is telling the story, but the final truth is that those of us who were changed either retreated into the oceans or were driven there, where we have lived ever since. We called ourselves Nereidis, which in our tongue means 'the people of the water'."

"Like the Nereids?" Dawn asked. "I've heard of them. Weren't they water spirits or something in Greek mythology?"

"Roman mythology, but yes," he replied. "Our language was old long before their empire rose, though. I don't know how they heard the word, but somehow our name became part of their folklore." Cijal shrugged and smiled down at her, trailing his fingers along the curve of her jaw. "There are so many things I've wanted to ask you that I couldn't before. You have these little markings here, across your cheeks and nose. What do these mean?"

"Markings?" Dawn asked, confused. "I don't have any markings, do I?"

"Yes, you do. On your face, and down here," he said, trailing his fingers down the side of her neck, across her shoulder, and down her arm. "These little spots?"

"Oh!" she gasped. "You mean my freckles? They don't mean anything, they're just pigmentation. Human skin changes colour if it's exposed to the sun for a while. Some people get a tan all over, but others just burn or get freckles."

"Freckles," he repeated the word slowly, as if trying it on for size. "That is a strange word. They do not teach us of such things in school."

"They probably don't think it's important," she replied with a shrug and a smile. "What about yours? Do yours mean something, or are they just cosmetic?"

"My markings?" He touched the side of his throat; suddenly, he looked self-conscious. "They are... yes, they mean something. Mostly to... females of my kind."

"Oh." Dawn paused for a second to digest that, then she glanced away. "So, they're a sex thing? Like, for attracting a mate?"

"Something like that," he replied, averting his gaze as well. "It is hard to explain. Female Nereidis are instinctively driven to look for the largest males with the most colourful and diverse markings."

"Yours are... very colourful," she commented, shooting a quick glance at him. "And you're really tall. Does that mean you're considered handsome by Nereidis standards?"

He gave her a sideways glance and a shy smile, but his only answer was a shrug. Dawn couldn't help but giggle. The answer was so obvious that she knew he was just being coy, but it still struck her as amusing. On a sudden, overwhelming impulse, she leaned up and hugged him as tightly as she could, relieved to have her friend back in her life at last.

***

They sat together on the beach and talked softly about nothing of any real importance for the rest of the afternoon, until the sun drifted down to caress the distant horizon. Finally, Cijal heaved a deep-throated sigh and looked at her reluctantly. "I must go. If I'm gone too late, my fellows will come looking for me."

"Of course, I wouldn't want you to get in trouble," Dawn replied, hiding the sadness she felt over his impending departure behind a smile. "Will you come back tomorrow?"

"Yes, in the afternoon," he said. "I'm expected to be in class in the morning, and if I'm missing it will raise suspicions." He sighed again, gently wrapping his arms around her. "I don't want to go. I wish I could take you with me."

"I know," she said, sliding her arms around his waist and resting her cheek against his chest. Amphibious or not, his body was warm and firm, and the contact stirred something primal within her. "But we'll see each other again. Tomorrow isn't very far away."

"True."

Cijal shifted within the circle of her arms. Expecting him to him to stand up and leave, she loosened her grip – but he didn't leave. Instead, he caught her chin with his fingers and gently tilted her face up towards his. Her heart skipped a beat when she realised that he intended to kiss her goodbye, and suddenly she felt a flash of panic. She'd never kissed anyone before.

As though sensing her nervousness, he hesitated. A moment later, his lips alighted on her cheek instead, feather-soft and unthreatening. Then he swept her into a gentle embrace and held her close, leaving her feeling disappointed and relieved in equal measures.

"Until tomorrow, my friend," he whispered in her ear, his breath warm enough to send a shiver down her spine. After a few long moments, he released her, rose to his feet, and walked down the beach to the water's edge.

Dawn watched him leave, feeling a strange combination of elation and despair. She hated to see him go back to the cold ocean all by himself, and yet the thought of seeing him again made her happy in a way that she'd never experienced before. As darkness began to settle in around her, she packed up her painting gear and climbed the dunes back to the house. There was light radiating from the windows when she got there. She opened the back door, and found Jessica standing at the stove, stirring something savoury-smelling in a pot.

Jess glanced up as she walked past, a surprised look on her face. "Oh, hey! I thought you were out."

"I was just down on the beach, painting. It's nice down there," she replied. It wasn't entirely a lie this time, and that made her feel a little less guilty than usual. Dawn set her equipment down by the door and seated herself at the table. "Did you make enough for two? I'm starving."

"Should be enough, yeah," Jessica said, glancing over her shoulder. She hesitated and raised a brow. "Dee, you're practically glowing. Did you get laid?"

"No!" she exclaimed. Embarrassed, she rubbed a hand across her face in an attempt to hide the flush that coloured her cheeks, but it was too late.

"Oh, yes you did," Jess cried gleefully. "Maybe you didn't get laid exactly, but you definitely met a guy." Leaving her cooking to simmer, she bounced over and sat down opposite Dawn, leaning against the edge of the table. "Come on, spill. I tell you all about my boyfriends."

"Yeah, but I never *ask* about your boyfriends," Dawn countered. "But... yes, I guess I did meet someone. Well, re-met. Is that even a word?"

"I don't care if it's a word or not," Jess replied. "I know what you mean. So, was it your long-lost friend, then?"

"Yes," Dawn said, looking down at her hands. "He's certainly a lot... taller than I remember. We were children the last time I saw him, but now he's all grown up."

"And so are you, last time I checked," Jessica pointed out.

"Yeah... I guess I am." Her cheeks felt like they were on fire. This was all new territory for her; she'd never been involved with anyone before. She'd watched Jessica tear through one boyfriend after another over the years, but she'd never had one of her own.

"Aw, look at you all shy," Jessica cooed, reaching over to tweak her cheek. "So, did he kiss you?"

"No," she said, rubbing her cheek anxiously. "But I think he wanted to. Maybe next time."

"Next time? So, he asked you out?" Jessica bounced up and down in her chair, clapping her hands. "That's awesome, Dee. Finally!" Suddenly, she went dead still and stared intently at her. "When are you seeing him again?"

"Um... tomorrow afternoon?" Dawn shifted uncomfortably, unnerved by the intensity of her best friend's gaze. "Why? It freaks me out when you stare at me like that."

"Tomorrow afternoon? Good, good... we've got some time, then." Jess steepled her fingers and narrowed her eyes at Dawn over the peak.

Dawn stared back at her, wondering what was going on in her best friend's strange mind. Jess said nothing, though, just gave her a mysterious smile.

Chapter 8

"Wakey-wakey, rise and shine!"

At daybreak the next morning, Dawn was jerked out of a deep sleep by a bellowing voice, followed a moment later by a human cannonball. Blankets and pillows went flying, tossed about by a rambunctious Jess.

"What? What's going on—argh, get off me!" Dawn protested sleepily, trying to shove her friend away. Unfortunately for her, while Jessica was a couple of inches shorter than her, she was substantially stronger. Before she quite knew what was going on, Dawn found herself dragged out of bed and shepherded into the bathroom.

"Shower time!" Jess cried. She shoved Dawn towards the shower, then scampered out and slammed the bathroom door closed behind her.

"Ugh, it's too early for games," Dawn complained, rattling the door handle fruitlessly, but Jessica held it closed from the other side. "Let me out, dammit!"

"No way, Dee. This is your first date, so we're going shopping," Jessica replied in a playful, sing-song tone. "We don't have much time, so hurry up! You don't want to keep your sweetheart waiting?"

"I don't— wait, what? Date?" Dawn blinked sleepily, staring at the closed door as though it would yield answers to her half-awake brain. "I'm not going on a date, am I?"

"You're going to hang out with a boy who wants to kiss you. That counts as a date," Jessica replied. "So, get your butt in the shower, and then we'll go buy you something pretty to wear. I'm going to go make breakfast, but don't you dare try to go back to bed. Promise me."

"Okay, okay, jeez. I'm showering, I'm showering." Dawn heaved a long-suffering sigh and stripped off her pyjamas. There was just no point in fighting about it. When Jessica got something into her head, you either helped her or got the hell out of her way.

Besides, she did want to look pretty... even if she didn't fully accept her afternoon liaison with an old friend as being a proper date.

***

Cijal stared thoughtfully into space. Learning was the last thing on his mind, even if he was in a human linguistics lesson. He was still in shock, and could hardly believe what had happened the day before was actually real.

His girl. His girl was alive, and she'd come back to him. It seemed too good to be true.

"What about you, Cijal?" the teacher asked, pointing at him. "What's an interesting human word you've learned this week?"

The question snapped his attention back to the present, and forced him to think fast. "Uh... 'freckle'. I learned the word 'freckle'."

"'Fre-ckle'? Is that English?" the teacher asked, picking up her dictionary pad. She flicked through the screens until she found the definition, then read it out loud to the class. "'A small patch of colouring on the skin that may become more pronounced through exposure to the sun.' How interesting. Very good, Cijal — I see you've been doing some extra reading."

Cijal just nodded and smiled. Yes, that was where he learned the word, through scholarly study and dedication to his craft. It had nothing to do with pretty human girls. Nothing whatsoever.

"All right, let's move along," the teacher said. "Today, we're going to read some classic human poetry. Despite their hostile natures, humans are very enamoured with the idea of romance and courtship, not unlike ourselves. I've uploaded today's text to your lecture pads, so please open the first sample."

Cijal glanced down at his lecture pad, swept his finger across the screen to wake it from sleep mode, and settled in for an hour of boring literary study. Just a few hours to go, then he could escape to pursue a little romance of his own.

***

"Oh, these are cute. What about these?" Jessica bounded over with a pair of pretty, strappy pink pumps in hand.

Dawn took the shoes and sat down to try them on. "These are adorable, but I'm meeting him on the beach, remember? They're not really going to work with that dress, either."

"You should get them anyway," Jessica advised solemnly. "This time you're meeting on the beach, but next time you might be going to a fancy restaurant. You never know when you'll need pretty shoes!" Without waiting for a reply, Jessica pirouetted on one heel and skipped off to find another pair.

"Jess, are you shopping vicariously through me again?" Dawn called after her.

"Maybe," Jessica replied, popping up over a rack of shoes. "But hey, give me a break here. Your skinny little size eight ass has no idea how painful it is to shop for a size eighteen. So, you just shut up and let me enjoy this. Today, you're my Barbie doll." With an evil cackle, Jessica vanished back behind the shelves, leaving Dawn shaking her head.

"How many times do I have to tell you that you look great?" Dawn protested. "Quit putting yourself down. "

Jessica muttered something incomprehensible and didn't reply. While she was busy searching for shoes, Dawn did up the straps of the little pink pumps and carefully rose to her feet. With delicate baby steps, she toddled over to a nearby mirror and posed a little, examining herself from a multitude of angles. They really were adorable. Perhaps she would get them anyway.

"I've got it!" Jess cried suddenly. With the same boundless energy that had powered her all morning, she raced back over with another pair of shoes clutched to her chest. "Goddess sandals. You shall wear goddess sandals. Yesssss."

"You're putting me in a white, empire-waist dress and goddess sandals? Are you trying to make me look like a Roman throwback?" Dawn asked, shooting her friend a dubious look. She sat down again and carefully undid the pink pumps, then put the sandals on instead. "Well, at least these things zip up the back. Doing up all those little buckles would be a pain."

"Look, I told you that you've got to trust me." Jess planted her hands on her hips and gave her a pointed look. "You suck at getting dressed up, and you know it."

"Know it? I said it," Dawn replied with a heavy sigh. "This is ridiculous. Just the other day I had to tell you that you can't wear work boots with a dress. It's like the blind leading the blind here."

"Oh, hush." Suddenly turning maternal and comforting, Jess plopped down on the bench beside her and rubbed her shoulder. "You're just nervous. You need to relax. He's just a boy."

"But he's not just a boy," she said, staring down at her feet. "He's a man. A young man, but still a man. He's just so grown up. I feel like a little girl next to him."

"Well, he must see something in you or he wouldn't be trying to kiss you," Jess pointed out. "So what is he, anyway?"

"What?" Dawn balked and stared at her, wide-eyed.

"What does he do?" Jess clarified. "Is he a student?"

"Oh." It took a second for the shock to pass, and for her to realise what Jessica was actually asking. "Oh! Oh, right. He's a… a cadet. I-in the Navy. A Navy cadet." It was an awkward lie and she knew it, but she couldn't think up a better one on the fly. To her relief, Jessica seemed content to accept the lie as truth.

"A boy in uniform? Me likey," Jess said with a nod of approval. "I'm going out tonight, so you two will have the house to yourself if you want it."

"Yeah?" Dawn echoed, glad for a change of subject. "Are you going out with Adam again?"

"Why yes, I am," Jess said. Suddenly, she looked very pleased with herself. "I'm at work this afternoon, and he's going to pick me up from the office. We're going to get some dinner, then go back to his house for a movie, and hopefully some snoo-snoo."

"Really, Jess? 'Snoo-snoo'?" Dawn asked, laughing. "What are you, five?"

Jessica folded her arms across her chest and tilted her nose up. "You heard me. There shall be snoo-snoo. Speaking of which, we should make sure you've got some condoms handy, too."

"Me?" Dawn yelped. "No way! There shall be no snoo-snoo on the first date, thank you."

"Hah-hah, made you blush," Jessica said teasingly, her smile turning wicked. Dawn suddenly realised that she was being twitted, and gave her friend a shove. Jess tumbled sideways off the bench with a dramatic wail, and rolled around on the floor feigning injury until they were both laughing so hard they couldn't speak.

***

"Oh, your name is Dawn — like the sunrise!" Cijal exclaimed, his expression lighting up. "Now I understand. You used to point west when you said that; I could never work out what you were trying to tell me."

"Hey, I was just a little kid," Dawn protested, laughing right along with him. "I didn't know the difference. All I knew was that my mummy named me after the sunrise."

Afternoon had come at last. Jess had gone to work a few hours earlier, leaving Dawn to get ready on her own. Although she felt a little silly getting dressed up to meet with one of her childhood friends, the look in his eyes when he saw her had made it all worthwhile. She felt very pretty and grown-up in her new white sundress and sandals, her hair pulled back in a neat ponytail.

Now, they sat side by side on a beach blanket in the shadow of her umbrella, just chatting about their childhood together. Cijal had changed a lot in seven years, and there was something very attractive about the man he'd become. Perhaps it was his exotic appearance, his gentle nature, his subtle sense of humour, or perhaps it was simply the fact that he was her oldest and most faithful friend. She felt a sense of trust towards him, and that was something that she'd never felt with anyone outside her own family. Even with Jessica, there was always that little voice in the back of her mind warning her to be cautious – but not with Cijal. She trusted him implicitly.

"It took me awhile to figure out your name, too," she admitted. "You used to get so mad when I called you 'boy'."

He grinned back at her and nodded. "I did. I was a very serious child."

"You really were. Shy, too. You used to hide from me all the time." She paused, tilting her head to look up at him. "You're not hiding now, though."

"Life is dangerous for a Nereidis child," he said, reaching out to trail his fingers across her shoulder with a tenderness that sent a shiver down her spine. "We are taught from the moment we're old enough to understand that we must hide from the unknown. In the ocean, even a small predator poses great risk to a curious child." He cleared his throat and smiled. "I was a naughty and exceptionally curious child."

"Why am I not surprised?" Dawn answered. She took his hand and smiled back. "You're being naughty by being here now, aren't you?"

"Yes, very much so," he said solemnly, his voice a deep, soft rumble. "If my people knew I was here, then I would be punished most severely." He lifted his free hand and gently ran his knuckle over the curve of her cheek. "I consider it a worthwhile risk. I have missed you very much, Dawn. You've grown into a beautiful young woman."

Dawn blinked owlishly, then looked down at her feet. "Thank you for the compliment, but I'm nothing special. I'm just... me."

"That's not true. You are very special." Cijal's voice took on a firm, commanding tone, one she hadn't heard from him before. His hand slipped beneath her chin, tilting her face up. "You're special to me. You have been for a very long time. Isn't that all that matters?"

His words were so intense that it made her heart twist in her chest, and sent another involuntary shiver down her spine. She swallowed hard, suddenly all jangling nerves and uncertainty.

"Cijal," she asked hesitantly. "Are you... in love with me? I mean, do you—"

"Yes." There wasn't even a second of hesitation between her question and his answer. Not the slightest bit of doubt. "I have been since I was a boy – it just took me some time to realise it." His eyes narrowed slightly, and his smile turned sly. "I'm surprised you'd ever doubt it. Why else would I have come so far, at such risk to my personal safety, to play with a little crystal-haired human girl?"

"Crystal-haired?" she echoed, making no attempt to hold back her surprised laugher; the merriment eased her tension just enough to bring her back into her comfort-zone. "I've never heard that before. Usually I just get called fire-wire or ginger. There was one kid who used to call me amber-pants, but... never crystal-haired. Is that how you thought of me?"

"Yes," he replied. "I was young and not as worldly as I am now. Your hair reminded me of the crystals that grow near my home." He captured a strand of her hair and twirled it around his fingers, as if admiring the colour. "My home colony is a city built in the heart of a sleeping volcano. Beneath our buildings, there are a series of smaller caverns, filled with pools of fresh water. These pools are heated by the volcano's blood until the water is pure enough to drink. Around the edges of those pools, beautiful crystals grow in great profusion. Most are deep purple, but some turn a bright orange colour when exposed to great heat." He paused, then gave her a sheepish smile. "I've never seen the thing you call fire, so I wouldn't know how it compares."

"You've never seen fire, ever?" Dawn stared at him wide-eyed, surprised by the revelation even though she knew she shouldn't be.

"I've seen the Deep Fires," he said. "That's what we call the volcano's blood, and that which oozes from the vents in the deepest part of the ocean — but no, I have never seen the fires that burn on land."

"I'll show you one day," Dawn promised. "Fire is strangely pretty, but destructive if you let it burn out of control. It's better to see it at night, though."

"I'll figure out a way to stay late one evening, so that you can show me," he said, nodding enthusiastically. "I would like to learn more about your people. What they teach young Watchers is very dry, as I am sure you can imagine. It gives little depth to your people."

"Why do you want to watch us, anyway?" she asked. "I mean, what are Watchers for?"

"Watchers are..." He hesitated, as though uncertain of the right words to use. "Protectors. We are not specifically observing your people, but watching the area surrounding our colony for any signs of danger. If we find any, it is our task to deflect it away. As a last resort, we are also defenders. There are often humans in our waters, but they rarely come close enough to be a concern. When they do, it is the job of the Watchers to lead them away."

"You don't kill them, do you?" she asked, concerned.

"No," he said quickly, shaking his head. "We only kill as an absolute last resort, and usually only when there's an immediate physical danger to our people, such as a swarm of sharks or stinging jellyfish. Your kind are usually more interested in the reefs. If they start coming too far in our direction, we use our allies to distract them. The humans already know our allies well, and find them fascinating."

"Your... allies?" she echoed, her concern replaced by curiosity again.

"Yes," he said. "We frequently ally with the other marine mammals who live in or near our territory."

"Wait," she said, holding up a hand to halt him. "You said 'the other marine mammals'. I thought you were an amphibian?"

"I am amphibious," he corrected, "but I am still a mammal. We are not natural creatures, so our physiology does not conform to the standards of the natural world.

"Oh." Dawn paused to consider that for a second, then she gestured for him to continue. "Sorry, what were you saying?"

"We frequently ally with the other marine mammals who live our colony," he said. "Usually it's the creatures you call dolphins and whales since we have a common language, but most of the others understand well enough to help if they're not available. In return, we offer them food, medical assistance, a place within the colony to warm themselves and their children during the cold season, or the use of our technology to locate better hunting grounds."

"Hold up again. You can talk to dolphins?" Dawn gasped. "So it *is* speech! Humans have been trying to decipher dolphin calls and whale songs for years, but we haven't had much luck."

"Definitely," he said, looking amused by her interest in his world. "There are a number of sub-dialects within each language, though, which would explain the difficulty your people have been having. We established a common dialect with them thousands of years ago, and we've been doing each other favours ever since. Our allies find it very funny that the land-walking humans do not understand their language, but the Nereidis do. They love to play with your kind, to see if you'll figure it out."

"Oh, wow," she breathed, overwhelmed by the connection between the world she knew and the one that only existed in her wildest dreams. "I feel kind of bad now. What about the dolphins in captivity? Aren't they angry about that?"

"Some of them are," he said with a shrug. "But most of them understand that a few of their people must be caged so that your people can grow as a species, to understand you are not alone in this world. It is my understanding that the dolphins in captivity feel they are ambassadors between their species and yours." Suddenly, he grinned. "I hear some of them actually prefer the lifestyle, since they get as much free food as they want and all they're expected to do is play, mate, and talk nonsense for the amusement of small human children. Not a bad deal, really."

"I never thought of it like that," Dawn admitted. "That is just amazing, though. I love dolphins."

"I passed a pod on the way here," Cijal offered, his eyes twinkling with obvious pleasure at her enthusiasm. "I can call them, if you'd like to meet them."

She stared at him, open-mouthed in surprise. "But... won't they tell on you for interacting with a human?"

"I doubt it. I've known the matron of that pod for years. She's a romantic at heart." His smile turned playful, and he reached up to cup her chin in his palm again. "If I tell her the real reason I'm here, then I'm sure she'll be more than happy to keep our secret."

Dawn looked up at him, staring deep into his stormy grey eyes as though seeking some hidden truth within them. "Then… you meant what you said before? About being in love with me?"

"Why would I lie about something like that?" he asked, raising a brow — or what passed for a brow amongst his species. Although his bone structure was nearly identical to that of a human man, his brow was hairless. Instead of follicles, delicately-tapered markings arched across his forehead to give the impression of brows when technically there were none.

"I don't know, I just—" Dawn stammered, lowering her eyes. "This whole thing just seems unreal, you know? The sweet boy from the sea returns as a handsome man, who tells me he loves me and sweeps me off my feet." She shot a glance at him, then looked back at the ground. "How do I know you're not just trying to… you know, snoo-snoo me? How do I know that you won't break my heart and go back to your pretty Nereidis girls?"

"I do not know this word, 'snoo-snoo'," Cijal said, his voice carrying an audible trace of concern. "But from your context I understand what you mean. However, I do not think you understand me. Dawn, my mother has been urging me to take a mate since I came of age last year, and I've been approached by numerous suitors. I rejected them all, regardless of how attractive or well-placed they were."

"Why?" she asked sharply, rubbing her cheek to try and hide her discomfort. When she finally looked at him, she found him looking uncertain and awkward.

"I don't know how to express myself better," he admitted softly, studying her with eyes that suddenly looked several shades darker, and infinitely sadder. "When you vanished, I feared you were dead, or that you'd decided you no longer wanted me in your life. I grieved for you, Dawn. For years. I came here every few days searching for you, but I only found strangers. I could not bear the thought of taking a wife when my heart belonged to someone else. It would have been cruel to her, and the thought of what it would do to me made me feel sick inside. At times, the despair I felt grew so potent that I considered going to the land and searching for you, even knowing that it would be suicide.

"Knowing that, imagine how I felt when I saw a face in the window of your old house. I came and I waited and I watched as often as I could, because I was not entirely certain it was you. Hope and dread have been a foul-tasting curdle in my belly for many days. It was only when you said my name was I finally certain that it was you and not a stranger who bore a passing resemblance to the child I adored in my youth."

Dawn stared at him, transfixed, as he told her his tale, afraid to move, afraid to blink, even when tears threatened her vision. When he stopped speaking and hung his head, she was left speechless. Never in her wildest dreams had she imagined that he would feel so strongly about her after such a long time. It seemed impossible for him to have missed her more than she'd missed him, and yet the expression on his face spoke of terrible pain.

"Oh, Cijal," she whispered the only words that she could think of. Emotion surged up in her chest with overwhelming strength, and instinct brushed aside all rational thought. With a muffled sob, she threw her arms around his neck and clung to him, trembling.

She felt gentle arms close around her as she wept, her tears rolling down his smooth skin to fall upon his thigh. Without asking permission, he gathered her up and drew her into his lap, holding her while she cried.

The fit passed swiftly this time, but she stayed where she was even once it was over, leaning against him with her head upon his chest.

"I-I'm sorry, I—" she tried to explain, but he cut her off by placing a finger against her lips.

"I know," he murmured. "You don't need to explain yourself to me. I share your pain." His hand shifted to touch her chin again, tipping her face up towards his once more. "The only thing I need you to tell me is if you feel the same way I do. Do you love me?"

"Yes," she said. "I don't think I realised it until recently. I could have done anything, anything in the whole world, but all I wanted to do was find you."

Cijal smiled at her words, but he didn't reply – at least, not verbally. Instead, he leaned down and kissed her. At first, it was so soft she barely knew what was happening; his lips were feather-light and so very tender. She froze, a thousand thoughts rampaging through her head. Her first kiss with a boy— no, a man. Her first real kiss. Panic flashed through her mind. What was she supposed to do?

Kiss him back, you idiot!

Jessica's imaginary voice chided her with such clarity that it almost made her laugh out loud. As always, Jessica was right, even if she was just a figment of Dawn's imagination this time. She closed her eyes and relaxed, leaning up into the kiss. She felt him relax as well, his nervous anxiety replaced by a quiet strength, and so much warmth that made her heart race.

By the time they parted, she was flushed and completely out of breath, but she was tingling all over in a way she'd never felt before. She opened her eyes and looked up at him, finding him in much the same condition: his eyes were lidded, and his grey-blue skin flushed around the throat and cheeks. She was fascinated, since she'd never seen him blush before.

In fact, she was so distracted that it took her a moment to realise that she could feel his arousal pressed against her hip. He didn't seem to notice, though, nor did he attempt to take things any further. She didn't know whether that stemmed from respect or uncertainty, but she suspected it was a combination of both.

Now that she knew neither of them had been with a lover before, she felt better. The relationship was new to them both, and where they chose to take it would be an experience that they shared and directed together. The idea pleased her immensely.

He was Cijal, after all. Her favourite boy. The nicest boy she'd ever met. Now, he was a man. A handsome, strong, gentle man who loved her. Dawn closed her eyes and snuggled close against him, silently loving him back.

Chapter 9

Dawn squealed with glee and ducked beneath a spray of water flung up by the tail of one of her new friends. The day after their first kiss, Cijal had arrived in the company of a pod of very playful bottlenose dolphins. It hadn't taken much effort to convince her to join them in the water.

Any nervousness Dawn might have felt about being in her swimsuit in front of her crush vanished the moment she realised that the pod included a pair of calves, sweet little twins no more than a few months old. They were shy around her at first, but once they got used to her they were happy to let her cuddle and play with them. One of the calves nudged her ankle, then popped up beside her, chattering gleefully.

"What's she saying?" Dawn asked Cijal.

"Nothing. She's too young to make much sense yet," he replied. Laughing, he ran an affectionate hand over the baby dolphin's head. "Think of it like baby-talk. Do human children baby-talk?"

"Oh yes, absolutely," she replied, she wrapped her arms around the wriggling calf. The creature squealed in delight and bumped her with her snout – then, suddenly, she snapped her jaw and bit Dawn's arm. It wasn't a hard bite but it was unexpected, and made Dawn yelp in surprise. A warning squawk from the pod's matriarch sent the calf fleeing, then adults gathered around her in a tight circle, trilling softly and nudging her with their snouts.

"It's okay, I'm all right," she tried to reassure them. She shot an appealing look at Cijal. "Could you please tell them that I'm fine? She didn't even break the skin. I don't want them to be mad at the baby."

"Of course," Cijal said. He let out a low, soft trill, a sound that echoed from somewhere deep in his chest or throat, and the dolphins responded immediately with a barrage of whistles and clicks.

"The matron wants me to apologise for her," Cijal said, switching back to English. "She says the babies are going through a phase. They're biting everything at the moment."

"Aw. Please tell her it's all right. Human babies do the same thing," she replied. "Oh, and please tell the baby that I'm not angry at her. I don't want her to think I'm mad."

Cijal's smile softened, and he conveyed her words to the dolphins. A few seconds after he finished, she found herself penned in by a pair of snugglesome calves, both making sounds that even she understood indicated contentment.

While she was distracted by the babies, the pod matron sidled up to Cijal and gave him a light thump with her snout. The sound of flesh on flesh and Cijal's grunt of surprise drew her attention away from the calves. The matron thumped him again, then opened her beak and let out a series of high-pitched trills. Suddenly, Cijal laughed.

"She's teasing me," he explained.

"What about?" Dawn asked, glancing back and forth between them.

"About you, actually," Cijal replied. "She says that you're soft and squishy, but pretty. She likes you."

Dawn paused to think that over, then she laughed.

"Well, I'm glad. You can tell her that I think she's pretty, too – and her babies are just beautiful," she said, hugging their firm little bodies. Somehow, when she thought of their chattering as baby talk, it made them even cuter. She clicked her tongue at them and made a few nonsense sounds, and they responded in kind.

Cijal laughed at their antics and translated her compliment to the matron. Suddenly, the babies squirmed out of her grip and swam away, then she found herself the recipient of a gentle nudge of the matron's snout. The big female let out one last trill, then suddenly she was gone as well.

"Aw!" Dawn cried, disappointed. She ducked under the water, hoping to catch one last glimpse, but the pod was already gone. When she popped back up again, she looked at Cijal. "I guess that last bit was her saying goodbye?"

"Yes," he replied, drawing up to her side with a few languid, easy strokes. "She said she has to go find some food for the little ones before the light is gone, and that she wished us both well."

"They're so beautiful," Dawn said, with a soft sigh of longing. "I almost wish I could go with them, and see what they're seeing now. It must be so amazing down there. Thank you for sharing a piece of your life with me, Cijal. I wish I could show you more of mine in return."

She reached out to him when he was close enough, feeling the warmth of his skin in contrast to the cool water. His arms slid around her, using his natural buoyancy to support them both.

"If only it were safe," he said, running a hand through her wet hair to stroke it back away from her face. "I am happy just to listen, though. We learn more about each other one little piece at a time, and that pleases me beyond words."

"True," she agreed. "We have time now. As much time as we can steal. I'm in no hurry. All that matters is that we're together."

"Agreed." His arms tightened around her, pulling her closer until their lips met in the softest of kisses, then he drew back and let out a sigh. "We should go back to shore. There's a shark coming this way."

"A shark?" Dawn squeaked. That one word was all he needed to say to get her moving; without waiting for another, she took off back towards shore as fast as she could go. Cijal was naturally a more powerful swimmer than she, but he deliberately trailed behind her to keep an eye out for danger from the deeps, and to give her a chance to scout the shoreline for danger on two legs.

She reached the beach ahead of him and paused amidst the breakers to check the beach for any uninvited guests. There were none. Cijal emerged from the water on her signal, and together they walked up the beach to where her umbrella and towels waited for them.

Dawn shot a stealthy glance at Cijal as she sat down, trying to gauge whether or not she should get dressed. He was hardly any more clothed than she was; his regular clothing consisted of only a pair of close-fitting shorts made of a thick, rubbery material nearly the same shade as his skin, which left his torso bare aside from a few necklaces around his throat.

She grabbed a towel to dry herself off, then suddenly she realised that he was watching her with interest. When she tried to catch his eye, he glanced away quickly, with the strangest expression she'd ever seen.

"What's with that face?" she asked.

"What face?" he said gruffly. "I do not understand your meaning." His gaze drifted down to the sand and stayed there, his big hands absently toying with the granules as though he were trying to distract himself.

"You've got a funny look on your face," she clarified. "Are you embarrassed?"

"No."

His answer was terse, and she knew straight away that he was lying.

"Yes, you are," she said, struggling not to laugh at his expense. "You're blushing. I know what it looks like when you blush now, and you're doing it. What's the matter?"

Cijal grunted and flicked a few pebbles away, sending them skipping across the glossy black sand. Then he glanced at her again, his stormy eyes showing a mixture of annoyance and amusement. "Your garments have become slightly translucent."

"What?" Dawn gasped. She squeaked inarticulately and clamped her arms across her chest. "Damn, I should have known better than to buy a white bikini."

Cijal cleared his throat awkwardly and muffled a chuckle behind a cough. "My apologies. I didn't notice until we left the water."

"It's okay, my fault," Dawn said, her cheeks burning as she leaned over to grab her cover-up from where she'd left it. She shook the sand out of it and was about to pull it on when a very different thought crossed her mind. She hesitated and glanced back at him. "I can put a shirt on... if you want me to."

"Ah—" He stalled, casting a sideways glance at her. "I do not particularly desire such a thing, no. But if you do not, then I may be compelled to look."

"What if I don't mind if you look?" she asked coyly, peeking up at him through a veil of lowered lashes. Although all of her instincts screamed in horror at the idea of being immodest in public, she lowered her arm slowly, giving him the opportunity to admire her if he wanted to. There was no one else around for miles in any direction, just the two of them. Even knowing that, she felt terribly naughty.

"You don't mind?" Cijal asked. His eyes lingered on her face for a moment, as though assessing her conviction, then they slowly drifted lower. The intensity of his gaze made her shiver, and she heard his sharp intake of breath and saw the flicker of desire pass across his face. When he finally spoke again, his voice was so deep and husky that it felt like a physical caress. "Dawn, I must tell you that I find you very beautiful."

"You do?" she echoed. Her cheeks burned and yet she felt strangely buoyant, fascinated by the power that she wielded. Suddenly feeling bold, she untied the back of her bikini and plucked the wet cloth away from her skin.

Her reward was immediate: he let out a deep-throated groan at the sight of her naked breasts. Even with a foot of space separating them, she could hear the quickening of his breath, and see the physical response that she'd caused.

She bit her lip and lowered her eyes for a moment, then glanced back up. "Would you like to touch them?"

"Yes," he said, his answer immediate and unhesitating. "And I would very much like to kiss you. May I?"

Dawn drew a deep breath to steady herself against the rush of desire she felt, triggered by the combination of his words and his expression. "Yes. Yes, please."

Moments later, a strong arm curled around her waist and swept her up into a kiss of such intensity that it snatched her breath away entirely. She felt her back touch the ground, but she barely even noticed. The hand that explored her bosom did not squeeze or grope, but stroked softly, so softly that it sent goose bumps up and down her body. While he kissed her, he trailed his fingertips around her ipples, exploring her curves with a fascination that almost bordered on worship.

Their lips parted and he gazed down at her.

"Your skin is so soft," he said, his voice little more than a murmur. She started to say something, but then his head dipped down and he planted a soft kiss against the arch of her throat. Then another, and another. Her words were forgotten, replaced by a gasp of pleasure. Cijal jerked back at the sound, startled. "Did I hurt you?"

"No," she whispered, slipping her arm around his neck to draw him back down atop her. "Do that again."

At first he resisted her, his confidence muddled by uncertainty, but something about the look on her face or the tone of her voice relaxed him. With a gentleness that belied his size, the young Nereidis eased himself down atop her again and he resumed pressing tender kisses against her throat. This time, he didn't pull away when she gasped, understanding the sound was one of pleasure, not pain.

He murmured a wordless response while he trailed his lips across her skin. Dawn closed her eyes, trapped between the sand and the ashen-grey body of the young man who had filled every one of her waking thoughts for as long as she could remember. She'd dreamt of moments like this, but somehow the reality managed to be so much more enjoyable.

Her head swam when his lips reached her breast and closed around one of her nipples, which he suckled upon with just enough firmness to send lightning bolts of pleasure all the way through her. She bit her lip to muffle her cry, but he still heard it, and this time the sound seemed to give him confidence. His hand left her breast and trailed lower, running down across her belly. A moment before his fingers would have slipped beneath the lower half of her bikini, he lifted his head to look up at her. "May I?"

"Yes please," she replied. Her entire body felt like it was on fire; she had no desire to resist what it wanted, and what it wanted was Cijal.

His fingers slipped beneath the thin cloth of her bathing suit and down between her thighs.

"Your body is slippery here," he said softly, his finger circling the tiny nub of her clitoris. "Amongst my people, if a woman becomes moist here, it means she... desires something. At least, that is what I am told."

"It— oh! It's the same amongst my people," she gasped. Even though his fingers did not delve too deeply, his touch was enough. When he smiled and pressed his lips against the curve of her throat again, it was just too much for her. She felt like she was going to explode.

It only took him a few minutes to bring her to the edge of climax, which he did with great enthusiasm. Her cry of pleasure startled him, but only for a second; once he understood what was happening, he relaxed and leaned close against her, guiding her through her orgasm with gentle fingers and soft kisses.

When she finally collapsed into a panting, shivering heap, Cijal eased himself down to lie beside her. He put his arms around her and held her quivering body close, but he made no attempt to coerce her into going further. Instinctively, Dawn understood that he was letting her choose the pace at which their relationship progressed, and she was grateful for it.

When the fog started to lift from her mind, Dawn opened her eyes and found him observing her with a peculiar mix of satisfaction and uncertainty. He touched her chin and kissed her softly, but said nothing. Dawn gave him her most radiant smile in return and snuggled against him.

As she did so, she realised that she could feel the swell of his arousal pressed against her inner thigh. She glanced down, wondering just how brave and bold she really was. With a deep breath to steady herself, she reached out and traced the shape of his swollen cock through the fabric.

His whole body stiffened at her touch. That surprised her, because the rubbery fabric was as thick as a wetsuit - she was amazed he could feel her at all. Suddenly, something clicked and she sat bolt upright.

"Cijal!" she cried, half-alarmed and half-worried. "These shorts are so tight, they must be hurting you."

Cijal shrugged and glanced away. "It's not so bad."

"Yes, it is," she scolded. "You flinched when I touched you. Take them off right now."

He looked at her wide-eyed, his expression one of total shock. "Amongst my people, it is considered a very intimate thing to allow a female to see you nude."

"That's not just a Nereidis thing," she replied. "Don't worry, Cijal. I trust you, and you can trust me. I'm already basically naked. Why don't you join me?"

"But..." He started to protest, but his words trailed off when she reached out to touch his stomach, trailing her fingertips across his skin. She could see him struggling to remain unaffected by her touch, but she felt his body respond. She bit her lip as she thought over her options, then leaned down and planted a soft kiss upon his stomach.

"It's just you and me here," she whispered, snuggled up against him. "There's no one else around. We can be comfortable together. I've never seen a man naked before, and I'd very much like you to be the first."

"I'm not certain that I am ready to take that step," he admitted.

"Okay," Dawn said simply. "I don't want you to do anything you're not comfortable with. All I want is for you to be happy."

She sighed contentedly and slid up along his body, to press her face against the curve of his neck. Despite the strange texture of his skin, it felt so right being close to him, like she'd finally found the place where she belonged.

Cijal didn't answer, but his touch was still tender and affectionate. She fell silent, content to wait patiently and let him take all the time he needed to think over his options. Eventually, she felt him begin to relax, but she didn't press him with questions or even look at him. She knew in her heart that her presence was enough.

A few more minutes passed, and then she felt his body shifting. When he finally stopped moving, she opened her eyes and looked up at him. He smiled back at her, the shy kind of smile that told her he appreciated her patience.

"You may look if you wish," he whispered, tracing a knuckle along her jawline. Then he kissed her, softly but briefly, a gesture of affection and trust.

A stab of painful uncertainty socked her in the gut. Only a few minutes earlier, she'd felt so certain that she wanted to see everything he had, but now she wasn't so sure. She squeezed her eyes closed for a second to gather her thoughts and recapture that impulsive sense of desire.

Finally, she took a deep breath and opened her eyes, guiding her gaze down along the length of his body. She followed his markings across his chest and stomach, and then down to his loins.

Her breath caught in her throat, and her voice came out as a startled whisper. "You're... so big."

"I am?" Cijal asked. Dawn nodded, but made no attempt to tear her gaze away from studying him. His markings criss-crossed his body in a delicate latticework that reminded her of some of the pictures she'd seen of tropical fish, and the effect was breathtakingly beautiful.

"Incredible," she murmured. "I think I understand why your females look for the most complex markings now. This is just... Cijal, you look magnificent."

"You are kind to say so," he said, his voice painfully neutral. "I've never considered myself to be any of those things, but I suppose it takes a lady to best judge my appearance."

Dawn looked up, searching his face for some clue to the way he was feeling. "Surely you've been told that you're handsome before?"

Cijal averted his gaze and shrugged. "Women have said so, but a compliment means nothing when it comes from someone whose opinion I do not care about. To hear it from you is different. I... I admit, I was worried that you would find me ugly."

"Ugly?" she echoed. "Why on earth would I think you're ugly?"

"Because we're different," he replied, reaching out to take her hand. He twined his fingers through hers and drew her hand up to his lips, placing a tender, reverent kiss on her knuckles. "We are so very different. Look here, at our skin. Yours is a beautiful, rosy pink, while I am dull and grey. How could you love someone so different?"

"Well, I do," she answered sharply, tears gathering in her eyes. "So don't even think like that. I don't care how different we are. I don't care what colour your skin is. I love you, and that's all that matters."

On an impulse driven by hearing the pain in his voice, she threw her arms around his neck and hugged him fiercely. The young Nereidis hesitated for a moment before he returned the embrace, but when he did it was with a firmness that said more than words ever could.

Chapter 10

"I should go soon," Cijal whispered, his lips close to her ear. "It's getting dark."

They'd spent the entire afternoon lost together, exploring one another's bodies with gentle touches and curious kisses. It was a day that had technically achieved nothing, and yet Dawn felt happier and more satisfied than she ever had before. Neither of them had suggested that they go all the way yet, despite his very obvious physical interest in her. Dawn was grateful for that, since it gave her time to organise her thoughts and work out exactly what she wanted her first time to be like. She was sure that she wanted it to be with him, but the exact details of where and when were still a mystery.

"Do you have to go?" she complained. "It feels like you just got here."

"Just got here? We've been together all day," Cijal pointed out, laughing. With a playfulness that contrasted against the silent stoicism of his youth, he grabbed her, pulled her closer, and lavished playful kisses up and down the curve of her throat. "I think you just want me to stay on the land forever."

Dawn gasped and shivered involuntarily, tilting her head back to give him better access to her neck. "Maybe I do, just so that you can do that all day and all night."

"Oh? You like that?" he teased. "I'll have to remember that for future reference."

"Aw, why did you stop?" she protested, feigning a pout. "Now you're just teasing me."

"Perhaps I am," he said, his voice dropping to a low purr. "How else will I make you long to see me again? I want you to dream of me this night, as I dream of you."

"I'm not sure you really want me to do that," she teased back, her eyes fluttering closed as he resumed pressing kisses against her throat. "If I spend too much time dreaming about you, then I'll have to figure out a way to keep you here forever."

She felt his heavy sigh, his breath hot across her skin. Worried that she'd upset him, she opened her eyes and studied him, trying to divine his mood.

"I don't want to go, either," he admitted, trailing a covetous hand across her body. His touch was so light that it almost tickled. Almost, but not quite. Instead, it left a sea of goose bumps all over her. "I just want to stay here and touch you forever. Your skin is so soft, and your scent so sweet. I fear I will be able to think of nothing else when we are separated."

"Good!" she said playfully, and gave him a tickle in a place that made him gasp. "Then I know you'll come back." Her humour faded away at the thought of spending yet another night without him. "I really wish you could stay over, even if we don't do anything more intimate than what we're doing right now. I miss you."

"I miss you, too," he replied, reluctantly withdrawing from her embrace. His powerful muscles gleamed beneath soft grey skin in the light of sunset as he sat up, then he looked down at her with a smile. "I hope I'll be able to arrange to stay one night soon. It is difficult. My people rarely leave home at night, and there are few people in my colony. It is problematic to arrange a deception when we all know one another."

"I'm sure you'll think of something," Dawn replied. She gave him a brilliant smile, and ran her hand up the side of his thigh and over his hip. "I would much rather have you in my bed than have to lie there all alone."

"Agreed," he rumbled. He grabbed her hand, drew it up to his lips, and planted a kiss upon her palm. "But... I must admit that I do like knowing that you think about me when you're all alone."

"Oh? You tease." Dawn sat up and leaned against him, to press a light kiss against his lips. "Do you think about me?"

"Yes," he admitted, his voice taking on the strange, deep tone that she'd come to associate with his arousal. His arm curled around her, and she found herself being drawn into his lap, where the evidence of his interest was most obvious. "Often. Sometimes even several times in one evening."

"Really? Several times?" she echoed. "Oh, my..."

"Mmhm..." His answer was a wordless murmur, punctuated by the tightening of his arms around her waist. All of a sudden, she found herself in a position that was blatantly suggestive, straddling his lap with her belly pressed firmly up against his. She could feel his cock between her legs, thick, swollen, and ready for her, yet he did not press for anything more. He just caught her chin with his hand and kissed her with such sweet, hot longing that it made her knees go weak. She found her body responding automatically, kissing him back, her arms around his shoulders, her spine arching to press her body against his.

"I have to go..." he groaned, his lips still so close against hers that she could taste his breath. Dawn whined inarticulately and kissed him again. Emboldened by desire, she slid a hand down between their bodies and trailed the tips of her fingers over his cock, tracing the thick, coloured veins that were his markings. Cijal's head rolled back, a guttural groan escaping from between his lips. He sounded so vulnerable, so pained by his need, that Dawn couldn't resist the urge to help him. She eased herself back until his thick cock stood erect between them.

"At least let me do it for you before you go," she whispered. Before he could answer, she wrapped her hands around his cock and began to caress him in long, slow, rhythmic strokes.

His protests died in his throat before they were even fully formed. Whatever he might have been trying to say was replaced by deep-throated sounds of pure, animal pleasure. She'd never heard a man make that kind of sound before, and it both fascinated and terrified her – but not nearly enough to make her want to stop.

By the time he finally came, the sun had nearly set and the first stars were sparkling in the sky above them. It was only when Cijal collapsed beneath her with a muffled cry that Dawn realised she could hardly see him against the dark grey of the sand.

"Oh - Cijal, you need to go," she told him, running a tender hand up across the exhausted youth's belly.

He was panting like he'd run a marathon, and his chest heaved with exertion, so it took a second before her words reached him. Suddenly, he sat bolt upright, but his voice was calm and showed no sign of regret. "Yes, I am quite late."

"Maybe you should tell your mother that you have a girlfriend in another colony," Dawn suggested, easing herself off him so that he could leave. "You said she was pestering you to find a mate... that might get her off your back."

"That's a very good idea, actually," Cijal replied, rising shakily to his feet. Dawn's breath caught in her throat as she watched him stretch, nude and magnificent, his skin edged with golden highlights in the last light of the setting sun. She bit her lip, her eyes following him while he retrieved his clothing and pulled it back on.

"Same time tomorrow?" she asked. The smile he gave her in return made her heart do a backflip in her chest.

"Of course. I wouldn't miss it for anything," he replied. He helped her up with gentle hands, then for a moment they stood together in the growing darkness, just enjoying one another's company.

"Cijal—" she started to remind him. He laughed and interrupted her with a kiss.

"I know, I know," he said when their lips parted. "I have to go. I'll see you tomorrow, my love."

With that one last farewell kiss, he released her and retreated into the water. Dawn shivered and hugged herself against the early evening breeze as she watched him wade out to waist deep, and dive beneath the breakers. Even when he was out of sight, he left her heart racing and her body quivering with longing.

"Yeah," she whispered to nobody. "I'll see you tomorrow. Come hell or high water."

***

Jessica was curled up on the couch watching television when Dawn let herself back in. She tried to sneak past without being noticed, but Jess took one look at her and reached for the remote. The television fell silent, leaving the two girls staring at one another.

"Well?" Jessica demanded.

"Well, what?" Dawn countered, avoiding eye-contact as best she could.

"Hey, stop trying to scooch away. You get back here and tell Auntie Jess your gossip," Jessica demanded, slapping the couch beside her. Dawn sighed; there would be no escaping with a half-hearted excuse tonight.

"There's no gossip," she protested weakly. She wandered over to the couch and plopped down, drawing her legs up to her chest.

"You're a terrible liar, Dee It's after dark, and you're dressed in nothing but a swimsuit and cover-up. I know something's up," Jess said dryly. She tossed the remote onto the coffee table and gave her a stern look. "I also know you want to talk about it. When I got my first boyfriend, he was all I could think about or talk about for weeks and weeks."

"I know, I was there," Dawn replied, staring down at her hands. She folded them in her lap and absently worried a corner of her cover-up, thinking over her options. Jess was right, in a way. She did want to talk about it with someone. It was difficult to go through her first relationship on her own, without her best friend knowing the full truth about her lover.

"Dee, what is it?" Jessica asked. "You look like someone kicked your kitten."

"I—" Dawn started to say something and stopped suddenly. Instinct warned her to be careful. It wasn't just her secret — it was Cijal's as well. Still, Jessica had never given her an actual reason not to trust her, beyond vague suspicions and gut instinct. They'd been close friends since they were thirteen. Would Jess really do anything to hurt her? She couldn't be sure, but who else could she trust? She had to trust someone. With that thought in mind, she drew a deep breath and looked up. "Jess... if I tell you a secret, will you promise me that you'll never tell another soul, ever?"

"Whoa, we're into the big secrets now?" Jess tilted her head and raised her eyebrows. "Of course, sweets. Is your new 'boyfriend' actually a girl?"

"What?" Dawn yelped. "No!"

"Oh, well, that's no fun," Jess said with a laugh. "So, what is it then? Is he a secret agent?"

"No, nothing like that," Dawn replied. "You're not even going to believe me. You'll think I'm crazy."

"I know you're crazy, honey," Jess said, patting her shoulder affectionately. "So tell me anyway."

Dawn shivered and stared down at her hands, twisting nervous fingers in the hem of her cover-up. "H-he's— I don't know how to say this. He's not human."

"Eh?" Jess tilted her head and wrinkled up her nose. "You mean he's, like, an animal? You don't strike me as the kind of person who gets off on bestiality, Dee."

"No! God, no – nothing like that." Dawn shook her head vigorously, embarrassed. Suddenly she found herself regretting that she'd said anything, but now she was committed. "He's a person. He's humanoid, but not... human."

"So... you're dating a Martian?" Jessica asked, her expression unreadable.

"No, not a Martian – well, sort of I guess, but at the same time, not." Frustrated, Dawn gestured with one hand out towards the ocean. "He said his people used to be human, but something happened thousands of years ago and they live under the sea now. He looks different to you and me, but he's still human in the ways that count."

"Wait, wait, let me get this straight," Jess interrupted. "This boy you've been seeing, he's a Sea-Martian?"

"Well, that's not what he calls himself," Dawn said with a nervous shrug. "His people call themselves the

Nereidis, like... sea spirits, but they're just people like us. His name is Cijal, and we've been friends since we were little kids. When I lived here with my parents, he used to sneak up onto the beach so we could hang out together. He's really sweet, Jess. I've never known anyone like him."

"I honestly can't tell if you're being serious right now," Jessica replied, scratching her head.

"I have never been more serious in my life, Jess," Dawn said. Her gaze flickered towards the muted television, but she stared through it without really seeing it. "God, I've never felt this way about anyone. I love him, I really do." Suddenly, a wistful smile danced across her lips. "And you should see him naked. Oh my goodness."

That comment quirked Jessica's interest. Her brows shot up and she gave her friend a sideways glance. "And you have? I thought you didn't need condoms because you weren't 'like that', missy!"

"We're not, yet – but I think we might be soon. We sort of, you know, played a little today," Dawn admitted. She could feel herself blushing, but this time she didn't mind. "I want to, but I'm not sure how to go about it. He still lives with his parents and has to go home at night. They'd be furious if they found out he was here with me."

Ever practical, Jess flicked her hair back and gave her friend a long-suffering look. "If Sea-Martians have parents, that means Sea-Martians can have children, so you should use protection. You don't want to get pregnant with a little Sea-Martian baby, do you?"

"Oh my god, you're so gross!" Dawn laughed and gave her friend a playful shove.

"Says she who's getting naked with Sea-Martians!" Jessica taunted, rolling onto her side to poke Dawn with her toes. After a few moments of tickling and teasing like children, she plopped her feet down in Dawn's lap and folded her hands behind her head. "So, what's he look like, then?"

"He's... I don't know, really hot," Dawn said. "He's really tall – I mean, *really* tall. Like six-foot-five, maybe? And he's all muscle. He's only a year or two older than me, but he doesn't look like a boy at all. I guess his people mature faster than ours do. He's got bluish-grey skin, and it's all covered in these cool colourful patterns."

"Grey skin?" Jessica echoed, wrinkling her nose. "That sounds kind of gross."

"It's not gross," Dawn protested. "Not at all. He looks like a human, except that he has different coloured skin. That's no different to me dating an African or Asian guy."

"He's a Sea-Martian. That's not the same as dating a black guy," Jessica said. "But I guess I can forgive him for that if he's, you know, built enough."

"He is," she said, ducking her head in a helpless attempt to hide her red cheeks. "He's big, Jess. Like, real big. I'm still a virgin – I'm actually a little nervous that it might hurt."

"Aw, it'll only hurt at first, if it hurts at all," Jess said. She eased her feet out of Dawn's lap and sat up straight so that she could put an arm around her reassuringly. "It hurts for some girls, but not all. If he's that big then ask him to, um, loosen things up a bit before he puts it inside you. Foreplay isn't just for fun. You'll be fine."

"Yeah, you're probably right," Dawn said, leaning against her for comfort and support. "It'll be his first time, too, but at least he doesn't have to worry about that."

"Well, if he's anything like a human guy, then he'll be just as nervous as you are," Jess reassured her, stroking her auburn curls the way a sister might. "Guys get just as anxious as you do, but about different things. Hell, he's probably more scared of hurting you than you are of being hurt."

"He was worried that I'd think he was ugly," Dawn said, resting her head against Jessica's shoulder. "I don't even understand how. Whatever species he is, he's the hottest guy I've ever seen. And he has no problems with performance, from what I can tell."

"From what you can tell?" Jessica echoed. "You mean, he...?"

"Yeah, we, um, touched each other," she admitted. "You know, like, exploring?"

"And?" Jessica prompted, giving her a light shake. "Did you like it?"

"Oh yes, very much," she said. "He made me, you know—"

"Use your words, Dee. He got you off?" Jessica supplied, never one to mince words on the topic of sex. Dawn just nodded. "Did he go down on you?" Jess prompted. Dawn shook her head, too shy to say the words. "What, with his fingers then?"

"Yeah," Dawn mumbled.

"Wow. That's pretty impressive for his first attempt. Are you sure he's a virgin?" Jessica sounded suspicious, but Dawn was too flustered to meet her friend's eye.

"Yes, I'm certain," she said. "He's really sweet. He's been waiting for me, Jess – since my parents died. Waiting for me to come back." Dawn sighed, the flush fading from her cheeks as she thought wistfully back to the happy times of her childhood. "The last time I saw him was right before the accident. That's why I *had* to come back here, and why I *had* to stay in this house. It was the only place where I had any chance of finding him."

"Aw. Well, I'm glad you found him again." Jess hugged her tight and gave her a kiss on the cheek. "If you need the house to yourself, you just say the word and I'll bugger off."

"I will," Dawn said. "I'm trying to convince him to stay the night, but he's worried about other humans seeing him besides me."

"I guess I would be too, if I were a Sea-Martian," Jess said. She smiled impishly and gave her a sideways hug. "The authorities would put him in a zoo or something, wouldn't they?"

"Yeah, or worse." Dawn agreed, then she extracted herself from her best friend's embrace and stood up. "I think I'm going to go have a shower and call it a night. It's been a long day."

"Okay. Goodnight, sweets," Jess said.

Dawn left feeling much better for having confided in her best friend, but what she didn't see was the look on Jessica's face after she'd left the room. If she had, she would have been a hell of a lot more worried, because she knew that look very, very well.

It was the look of human greed.

Chapter 11

Dawn woke the next morning bursting with life and creative energy. She bounced out of bed a few minutes after sunrise, fed herself a quick breakfast of fruit and cereal, then she grabbed her art bag and skipped down to the beach to wait for Cijal. Though she knew he wouldn't arrive before midday, she didn't mind the wait because it gave her time to channel her energy into an artistic bent. As she set up her umbrella and spread out her beach blanket, she marvelled at the way the soft black sand resembled his skin from certain angles. She decided that she liked his skin much better.

The painting she'd started a few days before was still unfinished; she hadn't felt the desire to pick up a brush again until today. Dawn mixed her paints carefully, choosing sunset colours for the sky and the water, pinks, purples, and soft blue-greys. Over the course of the next few hours, she put pigment to canvas and filled in the sweet colours of the early evening sky over the ocean. Eventually, she lost interest and started getting restless. With a soft sigh, she tossed her brushes into a jar of water and sat back, pondering what to do to fill in the last of the time before he joined her.

Another glance at the dark sand gave her a flash of inspiration. She dove into her art bag for her sketchpad and charcoals, and set to work on a new piece.

She was so wrapped up in her work that she didn't notice when Cijal arrived an hour later. It wasn't until she felt a body settle on the blanket beside her that she realised she was no longer alone. Her head jerked up and she stared at him wide-eyed.

"Goodness, you gave me a fright," she admitted, letting out a sharp, embarrassed breath.

"My apologies. I was making no attempt at stealth," Cijal said, his voice a deep, pleasant rumble. He kissed her by way of greeting, then looked down at her sketchpad curiously. "What's this?"

"Oh, just a doodle," she said, absently tucking a strand of hair back behind her ear. "I figured I'd work on my art while I was waiting."

"Is that me?" he asked. "It looks very much like me. How did you create this rendering?"

Dawn glanced down, a flush of pleasure rising in her cheeks at his praise. "It's charcoal, which is a special kind of ash that we make for art. Well, this kind is – there are a few different kinds of charcoal."

"Fascinating. My people have nothing like this," he murmured thoughtfully, reaching out to touch the sketch. Although his skin mostly resisted the water, he was still damp; when he touched the charcoal, it smudged and left a wet fingerprint on the paper. Cijal jerked his hand back, and his eyes widened. "Oh, I've ruined it. I apologise."

Dawn laughed and shook her head. "It's okay, it's only a sketch. I can make another one. It's just for fun."

"For fun?" he echoed, his tense expression relaxing when he realised that she wasn't angry with him. He glanced past her and pointed at her painting, which sat on a little easel, drying in the shade. "What about that? Did you create that, too?"

Dawn glanced at the painting and nodded. "Yes. That one's different, though. It's done in paint, which is a coloured liquid made with pigments. Please don't touch that one – you'll get paint all over yourself."

"Ah, coloured pigments," he repeated, nodding slowly. "My people use that in some of our garments and tattoos, but we can't create anything like this."

"I'm sure your people have their own kinds of art," she said. "Creativity is woven deep into the human spirit, and you were human once."

"That is very true, and yes we do." Cijal smiled and reached up to touch the necklaces he wore around his throat. "My people excel at literature, music, sculpture, and carvings. It is traditional amongst my people to add a new carving to your necklace at each major life event." He separated a few of the strands out and leaned forward to let her see the tiny, intricate charms that adorned them.

"Oh, I never noticed them," Dawn admitted, sitting up straight to get a better look. "So, each of them has some meaning to you? There aren't very many."

"I'm only young, I haven't had very many major life events yet," he explained, laughing. With careful fingers, he shifted the necklace around and pointed out a few different carvings as examples. "My parents made this one here for me when I was born, and my father gave me this one to celebrate my ascension to manhood. The rest of them mostly mark achievements in my schooling."

"What about this one, the one that looks like a little crab?" Dawn asked, reaching up to touch the charm in question. When she did, it slid aside to reveal a second, nearly identical carving on another strand beneath. "Oh, there are two. Why are there two?"

"Ah—" Cijal hesitated, suddenly looking flustered.

"What is it?" she asked, giving him a little nudge to encourage him.

"Well, ah, I—" Cijal glanced away, suddenly looking shy and nervous. "I made them last night, to commemorate finding you again. I was planning to give one of them to you. They are made from the crystals that grow near my home."

"Oh," Dawn said. It took a second for the full meaning of the gesture to sink in. "Oh! Because of the crabs we used to chase when we were children?" He nodded and gave her a nervous smile. Dawn threw her arms around his neck and hugged him tight. "Aw, Cijal — that's so sweet!"

"You'd be willing to wear it, then?" Cijal asked, sounding almost confused. "Amongst my people, it is considered intimate to wear a carving given to you by someone outside your family."

"I think I've already demonstrated how I feel about doing intimate things with you," Dawn said dryly. She pulled back, and touched her finger against the tip of his nose. "You're my not-so-little Sea-Martian."

"Sea-Martian?" he repeated. "I don't know this word."

Dawn hesitated, reluctant to admit that she'd told her best friend about him. "It's just a silly pet name. 'Martian' is a colloquial term for extra-terrestrials, which are a human myth — kind of like your people are to us. Martians are people that live on other planets and visit in space ships. Abduct people. Silly things like that."

The young Nereidis furrowed his brow, eyeing her uncertainly. "I am not sure I like this 'pet name'. My people have similar myths, but I am not a 'Martian'; I am a native of this planet, just as you are."

"That's why it's a joke," Dawn replied, giving him a reassuring squeeze and a kiss on the cheek. "Humans — other humans, not me — call anything that's different from themselves some variation of the word. Martian, alien, foreign. But if you don't like it, I won't call you that again."

"I would... prefer if you didn't," Cijal said, then gave her a shy smile. "I do appreciate the sentiment, though. Perhaps you could select another pet name instead?"

"Okay. I'll try and think of something." Dawn drew back and plopped down on her bottom with a laugh that was equal parts relieved and embarrassed. "Thinking up pet names is hard, though. I'll need some time."

"I understand," Cijal said, with a touch of amusement. He sorted through his necklaces until he found one of the strands that bore a little carved crab, undid the clasp, then he looked at her uncertainly.

Dawn just smiled and gathered her hair up in a knot, holding it out of the way. He seemed to understand the gesture without her needing to say anything. With gentle hands, he slipped the necklace around her throat and did the clasp up at the nape of her neck. For a moment afterwards, his hands lingered thoughtfully upon her shoulders. Dawn shot a coy glance over her shoulder, then let her curls tumble down, cascading over his hands like a river of auburn silk.

Cijal made an appreciative sound and snuggled up against her, burying his face in her hair. "Ah, you are so beautiful — my lovely, flame-haired maiden."

"You changed my pet name?" Dawn asked playfully, wriggling within the circle of his arms. With a soft, equally playful growl, Cijal drew her into his lap and hugged her tighter, murmuring affectionate nonsense into the curve of her neck. The feel of his breath upon her skin made her shiver and brought a flush of heat to her cheeks.

"Yes, I did," he whispered, nipping the tender flesh along the side of her throat with his teeth; his voice was so soft and deep it was almost a purr. "And I have another surprise for you, too."

"Oh?" she asked, equal parts alarmed and intrigued. So far, his surprises had proven to be... interesting.

"Your idea regarding what to tell my mother turned out to be quite insightful," he said, a smile dancing across his lips. "The next few days are rest days for my training group, so I have no obligations at home. I told my mother that I would be spending that time in another colony, courting a young lady."

"Courting a... oh!" She gasped and clapped her hands together in delight. "You mean you can stay tonight?"

"I can stay several nights, and I will not be missed," he said. "Unless you get tired of my company before then, of course."

"I don't think I'll ever get tired of you," Dawn said, laughing and throwing her arms around his neck to hug him as tight as she could — tight enough that he grunted and tickled her in revenge. She squealed and squirmed in his lap, fending off his big hands with light, playful slaps.

Then she found herself being kissed again, and she was happy for it. With the gusto of a starved woman at a buffet, she pushed herself up to her knees and straddled his lap, kissing him hungrily. His lips still tasted of salt water, but she didn't mind. Something about the way his skin reacted with the ocean made the taste just wonderful.

She felt one big hand creep up beneath the hem of her sundress, tracing the curve of her outer thigh.

Already flushed with the heat of desire, she made no attempt to stop it, not even when it snuck across her bottom and down between her thighs to tease her from behind. Cijal broke the kiss and stared down at her, his fingers roaming across the tender, sensitive outer edge of her labia, with just the thinnest layer of cotton separating their skin.

"You wear such fragile garments," he murmured, his voice a deep, silky rumble.

Before she could gather the breath to reply, his fingertips found the edge of her underwear and slipped beneath; her breath escaped as a gasp. Stroking her softly, he wrapped his other arm around her waist and drew her up against his chest.

"Hm, what is this?" he whispered, dipping his fingers between her thighs. "You're already as wet as the ocean, and I've barely even touched you."

"And you were worried that I'd think you were ugly," Dawn replied, laughing breathlessly. He paused and gave her an uncertain look that told her the comment was a little beyond the scope of his English just yet. "That was just a turn of phrase, a play on words. It's called sarcasm. I find you very sexy, Cijal. Very, very sexy."

"Ah." His expression relaxed, and he resumed pleasuring her. "Sexy, hm? I know this word. It is a colloquialism. It means that you find me appealing, does it not?"

"Oh, yes, yes it does," Dawn murmured, closing her eyes and leaning up against him. Despite his inexperience, his fingers were nimble, firm, and seemed to know all the right places to touch her.

"I would very much like to become more intimate with you," he told her, his breath stirring her hair. Her eyes fluttered open, and she found him watching her with an expression of contented laziness. "I think you would like to become more intimate with me, as well. Am I correct?"

Dawn gasped and buried her face in his chest again as his fingers swirled faster and faster across her most sensitive parts, teasing her into a frenzy. Her self-control was slipping away, but what little she had left was held in check by the tiny voice of fear in the back of her head. "Oh... oh! Yes, but... oh, God – please, stop for a second. I need to—"

His fingers stilled the moment she asked him to.

"What's wrong, my love?" he asked, his brow furrowing. "Did I hurt you?"

"N-no, but—" Even without the overwhelming distraction of his touch, she found herself having trouble catching her breath. Then, suddenly, tears welled up in her eyes. "I-I just—"

Cijal jumped and pulled his hands out from beneath her skirt, his concern turning to outright distress. "Do not cry, sweet one. I will never hurt you – never. If you don't want to be intimate, then I can wait. I would wait an eternity for you."

"It's not that," she said, swallowing hard and tilting her head back to stem the flow of tears. "I do want to, uh, be intimate with you – but you're so big that I'm... I'm scared it'll hurt if I try to take you all at once."

"All of these words I know, and yet I do not understand," he admitted softly.

"I know," she answered, closing her eyes for a moment to steady herself. "You're new at this, too. I just... I want us to take our time and enjoy this, okay?"

Cijal nodded gently, resting his hands upon her shoulders. "I am your humble servant, my love. Show me how to make you happy."

"Aw, it's not like that." His words brought the tears surging right back up again, but she forced them down again with stalwart determination. "We just need to take our time and be gentle with one another. I don't want it to hurt."

"And I do not want you to be hurt," Cijal said a heartbeat later. "I only wish to give you pleasure, as much pleasure as I am capable of giving. Tell me what I must do to erase this burden from your mind."

Dawn smiled at him, his kindness and determination to please reassuring her and driving away her fear. "Let's just keep doing what we were doing, and see where we end up. That seemed to be working pretty nicely."

He tilted his head quizzically, but this time he cottoned on much more swiftly. By the time she wrapped her arms around his neck and drew him down onto the blanket, he was grinning just as broadly.

Chapter 12

A few hours later, they lay side by side on their beach blanket, resting from their vigorous play. Thanks to Cijal's assistance, Dawn felt much better. He was gentle and incredibly patient, in no hurry to snatch away her maidenhood; just like her, he wanted everything to be as perfect as possible for their first time together. Dawn let out a soft, satisfied sigh, and rolled over on her side to rest her head upon his chest.

"Have I ever told you that you're very good with your hands?" she asked. With one lazy finger, she traced his markings all the way down his chest and across his belly. He drew a deep breath when her finger drifted lower, still following the same ridge.

Suddenly, he seemed to realise that she was talking to him, and let the breath out sharply. "Hm? Oh. No, you haven't, but I assumed my skill was passable."

"Passable? You're more than passable. Much more." Dawn laughed, trailing her finger around the shaft of his swollen cock, following the same vivid turquoise ridge. Even after two hours of love-play, he was still aroused and unsatisfied; for reasons he'd kept to himself, he'd decided that it was her time and he would enjoy no pleasure of his own until she was satisfied.

"Thank you," he said, running one hand through her hair. "I hope to be a fine lover for you, when the time comes."

"I know you will be," she replied. With a smile, she drew away from his hands and sat up; his eyes followed her with great interest, tracing the curves of her body with a hunger that felt so much like a physical caress. Struggling to ignore the way the feeling made her blush, she tucked her hair back behind her ear and smiled at him. "I want to ask you a question about your people. Would that be okay?"

"You've asked me many questions about my people already, and I've never complained before," he said. He raised a brow and stretched out, folding his hands behind his head. Dawn bit her lip as she watched him, handsome, languid, and massively powerful, almost like an overgrown, seafaring panther.

"It's a sex thing," she added to distract herself from the view. "I don't want to intrude on anything that's culturally sensitive."

"My people are very open about sexuality," he said. "Please, ask me anything – but my personal experience is limited, so I may not be able to answer."

"Well, let's try anyway," she said. "I'm curious about something. Do your people, um… perform oral sex on one another?"

Cijal blinked owlishly. "I do not know what that is, so I cannot tell you one way or another."

Dawn glanced away, focusing on her words to steady her nerves. "Well, it's when you use your lips and tongue to pleasure your partner. I know some cultures consider it taboo."

Cijal made a curious sound and fell silent for a few seconds, then he shrugged. "As far as I'm aware, my culture does not consider any act of pleasure to be taboo. There are taboos regarding who you mate with and who you breed with, but very few regarding the actual acts you perform with your lovers. But, as I said, I know very little about this thing of which you speak."

"Oh." Finding herself at a dead end, Dawn stared off towards the water trying to think of what to say next.

"You're more than welcome to show me, if you wish," Cijal offered. Though his voice was flat and emotionless, it was obvious that he was teasing her.

"Oh, you're so generous," she said dryly.

"More sarcasm?" Cijal said, feigning an injured look. "And here was I, trying to be gracious by letting you indulge your curiosity on my poor, hapless self."

Dawn laughed and gave him a playful shove, but he was unperturbed by the mock violence. He just gave her a knowing look and lay comfortably, waiting to see what she would do.

"Oh, you smirk now, but just wait and see," Dawn chided, then sat back to consider her options. She was curious, and despite his teasing it was clear that he was more than willing to be her victim. The idea was alien, but not repulsive. Quite the opposite, in fact – just thinking about it left a strange, excited tingling feeling in the pit of her stomach.

Tucking her hair back behind her ear, she shot a glance at Cijal's face. He was still watching her, relaxed but alert, waiting on her decision with a patience that outstripped his years. He just raised an eyebrow and said nothing.

"Ooh, stop looking at me like that!" she groaned, hiding her face in her hands. "I can't help being curious. I've never sucked a cock before, okay?"

Both his brows shot up this time. "Such language. Aren't some of those words considered to be bad?"

"Not really bad, just a little crass," she explained. She extended a finger and poked the body part in question.

"I think it depends on the context. Right now, it's totally fine for me to call that a cock. If we were fully clothed and in the company of other people, then it would be completely inappropriate."

"There is so much to learn about your culture," Cijal commented. He smiled at her – then, suddenly, he lashed out and caught her hand by the wrist, tugging her off balance until she slipped and almost fell on top of him. At the last moment, he caught her and pulled her in close. "So, do you wish to suck my cock or not, my love? If you tease it so, it will become distressed."

Dawn pushed herself back with a squeak of surprise and scrambled away from him, startled by his unexpected boldness. Cijal lay back again and folded his arms comfortably behind his head, an amused smile dancing across his lips.

"Oh, you're a bad one," Dawn teased. "Look at you, pretending to be innocent. I know better."

"I suppose you know better than any other," he agreed, watching her through half-lidded eyes, his demeanour now very deliberately relaxed and patient.

Dawn folded her arms across her chest and let out an indignant huff. "Fine then! I won't do it if you're going to be like that."

"It was your idea, my love," he pointed out.

Dawn paused and thought about it for a second, then she laughed. "Yes, I suppose you're right. All right, well... Just don't come crying to me if I'm terrible at this, okay?"

"I wouldn't dream of it," he replied, his expression softening. "I believe your people have a saying that would be appropriate here: 'Practice makes perfect'."

"True," she said, her mood brightened at the thought. "Practice is good. Lots and lots of practice.

Okay, but don't laugh at me." She laughed at herself instead, swept her hair back behind her head, and shifted herself into a better position to inspect his cock.

"Let me hold this for you, love," Cijal rumbled. Strong, gentle fingers took control of her hair, softly stroking it back away from the curve of her neck. Relieved of her burden, she still hesitated... until imaginary-Jessica snuck up behind her and smacked her in the back of the head.

Just do it, already!

Dawn almost laughed out loud at the voice in the back of her head, as clear as day. With tentative curiosity, she extended the tip of her tongue to taste the head of his cock. She half-expected it to taste awful, but it really didn't; a little bit salty, but mostly just like clean male skin.

She lifted her head to check on him, but he just gave her a reassuring smile. She smiled back and turned her attention back to exploring. There was no way she could hope to fit the whole thing into her mouth, but she was determined to try. Drawing a deep breath in through her nose, she eased herself down and slipped the first couple of inches of his thick cock into her mouth.

The cry that escaped from his throat almost startled the wits right out of her. Dawn jerked back and looked up at him, but it took a second for her to realise that it was a sound of pleasure, not pain. They exchanged shy smiles, and she resumed what she was doing.

His mask of impassiveness soon vanished as she experimented on him, sucking and nibbling this way and that, to discover the ways he most liked to be touched. Soon, he was writhing beneath her, his dignity lost in the face of the most intense pleasure that he'd ever known. The more vocal he became, the more encouraged she was. Soon, Dawn had the end of his cock buried as deep in her mouth as she could, her head bobbing in rhythm with his cries while her fingers explored the sensitive region around his sac.

As the minutes passed, his cries grew more frantic and she could feel him losing control. A small part of her was frightened of the demon she might unleash, but a larger part trusted him implicitly.

She was right to trust him. Even when the throes of orgasm overcame him, even when he tangled his fingers in her hair as his hot seed exploded deep in her mouth, he never hurt her in any way. Dawn closed her eyes and guided him through his orgasm, letting him vent his need inside her.

When he was finally done, she sat up and grabbed her water bottle to rinse her mouth out. For reasons she couldn't quite name, it felt slightly horrifying to kiss him without doing that first. Whatever else they might end up doing, she knew that she definitely wanted to kiss him again, preferably as many times as possible.

"Do we approve of that, then?" she asked, trailing her nails lightly across his chiseled abdomen. Cijal opened one eye and looked at her, his face a mixture of amusement and satisfaction.

"Yes, yes we do," he replied. "Do you also feel better now? You appeared rather anxious."

"I do feel better, thank you for asking," she said. "Speaking of anxiety, I think I should go check if anyone is home, so you can come inside. You must be hungry."

"Not yet, but I am sure I will be eventually." Cijal shrugged languidly and gave her a content smile. "I will wait here, then."

"Good," Dawn said, standing up to pull her clothing back on. "If I come back and you've vanished, I'll be very upset with you."

"Where would I go?" he replied. "Everything that I want is right here."

"Oh, aren't you the sweetest thing," she said, flushing with pleasure at his comment. "Stay here. I'll be back soon."

"Yes, my love," he replied obediently.

Dawn gave him one last smile, then she walked up the beach towards her home. The prospect of letting him inside both excited her and made her feel nervous at the same time. It would be nice to be protected from the elements and casual onlookers, but Cijal would be more vulnerable when he couldn't just vanish into the sea. She worried about him.

The porch creaked under her feet as she climbed the stairs and made her way inside. The back door was unlocked, just the way she'd left it when she'd gone down to the beach that morning. She crossed the living room to check the front door and found it locked. She called Jessica's name a few times, just in case. Nothing.

Reassured that the house was empty, she went into her bedroom and found her cell phone. There was a message from Jess waiting, a short note telling her that she was at work. Dawn thumbed a quick reply, advising her that she needed the house to herself for a while, then she put the phone down and hurried back to the beach.

By the time she got there, Cijal was dressed and sitting in the shade of their umbrella, waiting patiently. He stood when he saw her coming, the expression on his face a mirror of her own mixed emotions.

"It's safe," she told him. "The girl I live with is out. I've told her that I have a friend over, so she shouldn't come home unexpectedly."

"You live with another female?" Cijal asked, shooting her an odd look.

"Yes, she's my friend," she replied, kneeling to gather up her art equipment. "We've been friends for years. When I decided to come back here, she came along for the ride."

"Is she a threat to me?" Cijal asked softly.

"No, of course not," Dawn said. She shouldered her art bag, then leaned down to pick up her beach towel. With a flurry, she shook the sand out of it and folded it over her arm. "She's my best friend; she'd never hurt you."

"Ah, you misunderstand my meaning," Cijal said, shifting uncomfortably and watching her with unreadable grey eyes.

She glanced up at him, trying to divine his thoughts. When no answer was forthcoming, she gave up and asked him outright. "Then what do you mean?"

Cijal glanced away. The expression worried her; he rarely clammed up like that. She went over and stood in front of him, trying to catch his eye. "Cijal? Talk to me. I can't answer you if you won't tell me what's wrong."

He sighed heavily and his shoulders slumped. "I mean, is she a threat to my position... with you?"

Dawn stared at him, turning his words over in her head. Suddenly, the pieces fell into place and her eyes widened.

"You think she's my girlfriend?" she blurted, shocked and a little scandalised by the suggestion. "No way! I'm not into girls. I mean, not like that."

"Oh." Cijal looked so relieved that for a moment she was afraid he was going to fall over. "I'm sorry, I didn't know. I worried that I would be competing for your affections."

"You're not," she repeated firmly, shaking her head. "You're the only one I've ever been involved with – emotionally, physically, or sexually."

"I understand. I'm sorry for my assumption." He drew a deep breath and reached out to touch her arm. There was an awkward pause, then he gestured towards her armload. "May I aid you with that?"

"No, it's okay. My art gear is kind of fragile, I'd rather carry it," she replied. "Come on, let's go inside. It looks like rain."

"What does?" he asked, looking around in obvious confusion.

Dawn laughed. She folded the beach umbrella down, then picked it up and offered it to him. "The sky looks like rain. You see how grey the clouds are? That means it's probably going to rain soon. It's been a dry summer, so we could use some rain."

"Rain is water that falls from the sky, yes?" Cijal asked. He took the umbrella and looked up at the clouds with great interest. "I've seen it before, but we have no name for such a concept."

"Well, I suppose you wouldn't need to," she said. She shifted her art gear into the crook of her arm and took his hand. "It doesn't rain under the sea."

"No, but it rains *on* the sea," he replied. "We have words for the phenomena it spawns, but not for the actual event itself. Our words describe the way it brings the fish near the surface to feed, so our hunters may strike them easily, and we have other words to describe how the sea becomes rough and difficult to swim through when then sky rages overhead."

"Ah, storms," Dawn said, nodding. "I never thought about how a storm at sea would affect your people. It must be dangerous."

"Yes," he said, frowning. "We usually stay in our colony when the sky is angered. Sometimes the earth trembles beneath the waves, and destruction is unleashed upon us. Some years ago, a terrible wave destroyed one of our distant colonies. Many of my people died – and yours as well. My father and brother both travelled away for weeks to help in the wake of that disaster. When they returned, they told me that there were thousands of bodies in the water, human and Nereidis alike."

"Oh my God. That must have been terrifying." Dawn shivered and cuddled up against his side, suddenly feeling cold despite the summer warmth. "Now I'm never going to stop worrying about you. Let's talk about something else."

"As you wish." Cijal laughed, his mood lightening immediately. Hand in hand, they began to walk towards the beach house. "I am excited to see the inside of your home. I must admit that I've wondered about it many times over the years."

"I know how you feel," she replied. "I always wondered where you went when you vanished into the water."

Conversation halted for a moment as they cleared the crest of the dune and made their way towards the old porch. The boards creaked softly under Dawn's feet again as she mounted the stairs. Behind her, Cijal hesitated.

"We live in caverns deep beneath the waves," Cijal said, looking around himself curiously. He lifted a hand to touch the frame of the porch, trailing his fingers across the rough, unsealed wood. "Our colonies are nothing like this. We carve them out of the rock, and use our technology to light them and fill them with air."

"That's wood," she said, supplying the answer to the question before he even asked it.

"Ah, I know that word." Cijal glanced at her, his eyes alight with interest. "Wood is the meat from trees, yes?"

"That's one way to put it, yes." Struggling not to laugh at the image his words conjured, she leaned over and tapped the weatherboard beside the front door. "This is wood, too, but it's been painted. We sometimes build with stone, but mostly we use timber, brick and concrete."

"Most interesting," Cijal replied, moving up beside her to run his fingers across the wall beside her hand. Once his curiosity was sated, he placed a gentle hand on her waist and glanced past her. "This is the door, I know that much. I've seen you come and go through it." He tilted his chin towards the door, then looked down at her. "May we go in?"

"Yes, we may," she replied. With a flourish, she opened the back door and led him into her home for the very first time.

Chapter 13

Dawn and Cijal spent the next few hours wrapped up in questions and answers. Cijal was fascinated by every aspect of her home and her culture, and in return he offered her insight into his life beneath the waves. Seeing her world vicariously through his eyes was a fascinating experience for her; some of the things she considered to be ordinary, boring, everyday objects were completely new and amazing to him.

Television was one of those things. While Dawn was preparing dinner, Cijal sat in front of the television, completely enraptured by the sights and sounds.

"You really don't have television?" she asked. "I'm still struggling to wrap my head around that. What do you do for fun?"

"We have many things, but nothing like this," he replied. "We have computers and books, though they are very different to the ones you showed me earlier. The elders frown on the use technology for personal entertainment, so we spend most of our free time with friends. Sometimes we make music and dance, sometimes we create sculptures together, sometimes we... I do not remember the word. When you compete against one another in physical competition?"

"Sports?" she supplied.

"Yes, sports," he said. "We enjoy sports. Everyone has different preferences, though. Some like to travel and see the world, some prefer to stay home and create things, or write books. Some prefer to be alone, while others like to have company. There are as many options as there are people."

"That sounds nice," Dawn admitted. She paused in her cooking and shot a worried look at him. "Are you sure you don't have any special dietary requirements?"

He shook his head and gave her a wry smile. "I'm fairly certain that I'm capable of digesting the same things you are. Don't be concerned, my love; I'm looking forward to sampling your cuisine."

"'Cuisine' may not be the right word to describe my cooking," she said, her voice heavy with sarcasm. "Honestly, I just consider it a win if no one dies."

"That sounds promising," Cijal said, laughing. He picked up the remote control and stared at it, then delicately pushed a button to change the channel, just as she'd shown him.

Loud rock music blared from the television. Cijal almost jumped out of his skin, then frantically mashed buttons on the remote until the noise went away.

"That was awful," he said. "What was that?"

"Music," she explained. "Or at least, what some humans call music. It's not all like that. Like you said, different tastes for different people."

"My people also make music – but not like that." The youth shot a dubious look at the television, only to get distracted again. The conversation trailed off while Cijal sat entranced, giving Dawn the time she needed to finish off their dinner. She divided her offerings onto plates, then picked them up and carried them into the living room to see what had him so fascinated.

"Oh dear," she said when she caught sight of the screen. "You're in for disappointment if you think that's how I cook."

Cijal glanced up and frowned at her. "Don't say that, my love. Nothing you could do would ever disappoint me."

"I think you should reserve judgement until after you've tried my bangers and mash," she said. She handed him one of the plates and a set of utensils, then she sat down beside him.

Cijal stared at his food, looking intrigued but uncertain. "I don't know how to eat this."

"Just watch what I do," she told him. "Don't worry, it's not hard."

What began as an innocent lesson in human dinner etiquette swiftly dissolved into a messy rendition of what not to do with a knife and fork. By the time they'd finished eating, Dawn was laughing so hard she could barely swallow, and poor Cijal was splattered from head to toe with tomato sauce and mashed potato.

"Good lord, it's like teaching a two-year-old," Dawn managed to gasp between fits of laughter. Cijal shot her a wounded look, but she could see him struggling to hide a smile. Once they finished, Dawn rose from her seat to confiscate his dirty dishes.

"It is not my fault. I'm used to different fare," Cijal protested. He rose as she went back to the kitchen and followed her. "I fear I must bathe, though. Do humans keep facilities for such things?"

"Of course," she said as she set the dishes in the sink, then turned back to face him. "It's fresh water, though. You can run it hot or cold, depending on your preference."

He smiled at her and reached up to touch her cheek, his big thumb leaving a tiny smear of tomato sauce on her skin. "My people bathe in fresh water as well, and most of us prefer it warm. That's why we build our homes around the undersea vents. The magma makes it easier to heat and filter the water."

"You know, I did wonder about that," Dawn admitted. She grinned and took his hand, leading him towards the bathroom. "I mean, you live in the water and the sea isn't a very clean place, but you never smell grungy."

"Technically, we live *under* the water, not in it," he said. "Our caverns are sealed pockets of air. We're comfortable in the ocean – we farm in it, play in it, and we travel through it often, but we don't actually live in it. We can breathe the water for a time, but eventually we do need air."

Dawn glanced over her shoulder and gave him a shy smile. "Your home sounds fascinating. I'd love to see it one day."

Cijal smiled back, but she could see the uncertainty in his eyes. "Perhaps one day. I fear my elders would be no more accepting of you than your parents would have been of me."

"That's a shame. Good thing we can form our own opinions, huh?" With a playful giggle, she dragged Cijal into the bathroom and closed the door behind him. "Take off your clothes. Let's give them something to really disapprove of."

Cijal's brows shot up. "What are you planning, my little flame-haired maiden?"

"To not be a maiden anymore," she said bluntly, then she stripped off her dress and underwear, dropping them in a heap on the floor. "If you want to, that is. I mean, let's have a bath and see where the mood takes us."

"Hrrrm," Cijal mumbled thoughtfully, his voice little more than an inarticulate purr. "It almost sounds like you planned this, my love. Is that why you fed me such messy food?"

"No!" Dawn protested, laughing. "I swear, I didn't know that you'd end up wearing half your dinner."

With a wink, she bounced past him and swept aside the curtain, to switch the shower on. Water exploded from the shower head, and behind her she heard Cijal grunt in surprise. She glanced back over her shoulder and found him staring at the stream of droplets curiously.

"This is how you bathe?" he asked. "I expected a pool of some kind."

"We do that sometimes, but showers are faster and fit in smaller spaces," she explained. Once the shower was warm enough, she stepped beneath the stream. Water cascaded down over her in a steamy caress, but the shiver that ran through her had nothing to do with that. The thought of a man watching her in the shower still felt so wrong, and yet so very, very right.

A large body joined her a moment later and she felt his hands alight upon her hips. His eyes roamed across her body, following the flow of the water as it rippled over her skin. There was a peculiar little smile upon his lips, and his expression was one of such rapt fascination that Dawn felt her loins tighten in response.

"Hmm," he growled deep in his throat, a low, animal noise of appreciation. "Suddenly, I understand the appeal."

"Then why do you still have your shorts on?" she asked, closing the space between them to press her belly up against his. Her arms slid around his waist and down the back of his shorts to stroke the curve of his buttocks.

Cijal grunted in surprise, but he looked more pleased than annoyed. "Well, I'm not dirty under there."

"Yes, you are," Dawn whispered teasingly, leaning up on tiptoes to press a kiss against the side of his neck. She slipped her thumbs into what passed for the waistband of his shorts and eased them down off his hips. Though she half expected him to protest about intimacy again, this time he said nothing. He stood as still as a statue while she slipped the fabric all the way down his legs, until it pooled around his ankles. When she straightened up again she was drenched, her long hair plastered to the sides of her head, and her supple young body slippery and wet. She ran her hands back through her hair to push it out of her face and looked up at him.

"Isn't that so much better?" she asked softly, her voice barely audible over the noise of the water. Cijal glanced down, first at himself and then at her.

"It certainly does seem to be," he agreed, kicking his shorts into a corner of the shower box. His strong, gentle hands fell on her hips again, but this time they didn't just rest there. This time, he pulled her up against his body and there was something firm in his touch, something commanding, perhaps even a little demandingly. She felt like she should have been afraid of the strength in his hands, she wasn't; to her surprise, she realised that she liked it.

Cijal leaned down and caught her lips in a kiss of such heat and passion that she went weak at the knees. By the time he broke it, she was quivering all over and gasping for breath. In a half-hearted attempt to keep the illusion of self-control intact, she fumbled for the little shelf in the corner where she kept a bar of soap and a washcloth. He watched her with interest, his eyes following her hands as she soaked the cloth and began to wash him.

Dawn found herself struggling to breathe, aroused beyond all reason by the simple act of showering with a lover. Suddenly, the term 'steamy' made sense to her. The moment was so very steamy, and it had nothing at all to do with the billowing vapour all around them. As her washcloth moved lower, she realised that she was not the only one affected.

Suddenly, Cijal stepped forward and pinned her up against the wall with his body, his hands firm but always gentle. With a soft sound of animal desire, he lowered his head to the curve of her neck and planted a few tender kisses upon her skin. Dawn gasped, and the soap slipped from her fingers, vanishing into the turbulent water around their feet.

"I want you to tell me something," he murmured, his hands roaming over her, caressing her slippery curves. The water cascaded over his broad shoulders and back, leaving only a few delicate droplets to pitter-patter over her – but despite that, she wasn't cold.

"Anything," she whispered breathlessly. Desire twisted her belly with an intensity that was almost painful. Her body longed for him, for every part of him, for every inch of the swollen cock pressed up against her.

"I want to hear your words," he said, his voice a deep growl from lips pressed right against her ear. "My people have special words, shared only between lovers in moments of intimacy. They did not teach me such things in your language, so I want to hear them from you."

"You... you want me to talk dirty to you?" she replied. Her mind raced, and yet she ended up drawing a blank. Then one strong arm clamped around her waist and drew her stomach up hard against his, their bodies sliding together slick and slippery-wet. Suddenly, all of her thoughts were dirty. "We call it, um— there are a lot of different words. Sometimes, we say that we want to make love."

"Mm, that is a pleasant term," he purred, nuzzling her, his lips pressed against her tender throat in a way that made her heart race and her skin tingle. "What does this one mean?"

"It's—ah, it's gentle," she said, struggling to assemble some kind of coherent answer. "Making love is like curling up in lover's arms and falling gently into passion."

"Hm. Fascinating," he said, his lips leaving a trail of feather-soft kisses along her throat. "Tell me more. What other words are there?"

Dawn closed her eyes and slid her arms around his shoulders, her fingers toying with his glossy white hair. "Well, sometimes you don't want your lover to be so gentle, so then you say, 'I want you to fuck me, Cijal. I want you to pin me up against this wall and ravish me.'"

Cijal drew back just enough to fix her with a curious look. "Were you asking me or telling me?"

"Asking you," she replied, then she leaned up and kissed him hard. A few seconds later, she pulled back and looked him straight in the eye. "I've been waiting for you my whole life, Cijal. I want you to fuck me until I can't walk straight." She paused, her heart still racing and her chest heaving – then she flashed him a winning smile. "Please?"

A deep-throated growl was her only answer, and then she found herself swept off her feet and pinned against the wall of the shower stall. His big hands were gentle but not timid as he guided her legs up to wrap around his waist. All the shy uncertainty she'd seen in their first few days of play was gone, replaced by a confidence that made her quiver.

He supported all her weight with a single hand upon her bottom, while he slid the other hand down between them and took his cock in hand. He guided the engorged head up between her thighs and glanced up at her, poised on the very edge of a precipice from which neither of them could return.

"This is your last chance, my love," he reminded her, his voice soft and his expression a mixture of adoration and lust. "If you've changed your mind, speak now; I won't hold it against you."

"I won't change my mind. I want it, Cijal—I want you," she replied, then she hugged him and kissed him hard.

A moment later, her world just about exploded.

He was not rough on that first thrust, but he was not entirely gentle either. Bracing himself against the wall with one hand, he eased his thick cock into her, slowly, slowly, letting her feel every inch. Pleasure erupted through her as it stretched her for the very first time, but it was not just his girth that made her suffer the throes of such impossible ecstasy – it was that intricate web of ridges that adorned his entire shaft, courtesy of his markings. It was like nothing she'd ever imagined. Exquisite pleasure exploded within her and radiated out to the very tips of her limbs – but that was only the beginning. Once he was fully mounted, his instincts took over. He kissed her hard, and then their passion began in earnest.

The hot water left both of their bodies slick and lubricated their sex. The moment Cijal realised that she wasn't in pain, his lust was unleashed. He thrust himself deep inside her, again and again, and lavished her lips and throat with frantic kisses. She clung to him, her inarticulate sobs of appreciation insufficient to express the way she felt, but somehow he understood.

With a soft grunt, he shifted his grip and braced both hands beneath her bottom, to give himself better leverage. The change of position was only slight, but the ecstasy was so intense that it left her seeing stars. She didn't have time to comment or even think about it — she was on the verge of orgasm, and the shift pushed her over the edge. The tendrils of exquisite pleasure wrapped themselves around her belly and squeezed hard, making her cry out unabashedly. Her back arched and her limbs trembled, but Cijal barely even seemed to notice. His only acknowledgement was a soft growl, but after so many years of waiting and wondering, he wasn't finished with her so soon.

Eventually the hot water ran out, but that didn't matter. With single-minded determination, he wrapped his arms around her and carried her out of the bathroom. He took her to bed, a bed she'd shown him earlier with such coyness. There, he lay her down on top of the duvet and eased himself back into her. With the thirst of a dying man, he kissed her and kissed her; she responded in kind, wrapping her arms and legs around him.

The second orgasm that he drew from her took longer, but it was so much more luxurious. Eventually his thrusts faded from hot and frantic to slow and sensual, and yet they still left her breathless and quivering with ecstasy. Neither of them noticed when the light began to fade and the room filled with evening gloom, both lost in a world shared only by two.

It might have been as much as an hour, perhaps even more, but Dawn lost all concept of time when he was within her. Only his touch mattered, the feel of his lips upon her skin, and his cock within her. After that first, earth-shattering orgasm, it was hard to think of anything at all except for him. By the time his thrusts finally began to grow uneven and his breath became ragged beside her ear, she was bordering on exhaustion.

"I am going to... I-I..." he whispered, his harsh breathing making it difficult for him to speak. "I... I don't know the word..."

"Come. You're going to come," Dawn supplied. He made an inarticulate sound of understanding and gripped her tight, his big hands digging into her skin. For the first time, she felt pain – but it was a good kind of pain and didn't bother her. She hugged him tight in return and held him close. He kissed her with all his might, and his eyes fell closed. With one last thrust, he embedded his cock deep within her and finally succumbed to his own release.

Eventually, after what felt like forever but was in reality only a few seconds, he collapsed atop her. Even exhausted, he maintained enough presence of mind not to crush her beneath the weight of his much larger body. He rolled onto his back and drew her atop him, so that she could snuggle comfortably against his chest.

And snuggle she did. For the first time in her life, Dawn felt truly satisfied. Even their moments of love-play did not compare to the final act of consummation. As they lay together silently in the dark, her body was still trembling with exertion, twitching and shivering beyond her control.

Cijal recovered more quickly. After a few minutes, he opened his eyes and looked at her, his face barely visible in the shadows.

"So, was it as bad as you feared?" he asked.

"No," she replied. "It was better than I ever dreamed it could be – and it didn't hurt at all." She managed an exhausted giggle, but her body craved sleep and she was more than happy to give in and let it have what it wanted.

The last thing she heard before she drifted off was Cijal's soft, pleased chuckle, and that sound made her happy.

Chapter 14

At some point during the night, they woke long enough to dry themselves off and strip the wet duvet off the bed. A sheet was more than enough to keep them comfortable on a warm summer night, especially when they had one another. Once she was dry, Dawn snuggled back into the crook of Cijal's arm and quickly tumbled into a deep, contented sleep.

Just after sunrise, the soft patter of rain on the roof woke her. She lay in a blissful doze for a few minutes, until she felt Cijal shift ever so slightly beneath her. She opened her eyes and found him wide awake and watching her,

"Good morning," he said, trailing one knuckle the length of her jaw. He gave the kind of smile that made her stomach twist, then he kissed her. She closed her eyes to enjoy it, until a horrid realisation struck her.

"Wait!" she yelped, shoving herself away from him. "Don't kiss me yet!"

"What?" Cijal jumped and stared at her, bewildered by her rejection. "What did I do wrong?"

"Nothing, nothing at all. I'll be back in a second." Dawn rolled out of bed, raced into the bathroom, and just about set a new land speed record for racing through her morning ablutions. Once she was washed, groomed, and relieved, she hurried back out to her bedroom.

Cijal was sitting in bed waiting for her, staring at the bathroom door with a look of profound confusion. The moment it opened, his expression brightened.

"Sorry, that was all me," she admitted, sitting down beside him. "I'd hate for you to have to put up with my smelly morning breath."

"You are anything but malodorous, my love," he told her. His arms closed around her, and she found herself being kissed all over again. This time, she relaxed into it and let it linger for as long as he wanted it to. He seemed to be immune to morning breath; his lips tasted just as wonderful first thing in the morning as they had the night before.

Thinking about that brought with it memories of their tryst, right there in that bed. She was no longer a virgin, and neither was he. Her body ached in places that were new to her, and yet it wasn't a bad kind of ache. It was the kind of ache that made her long for more... once she'd had time to recover from the first round.

Dawn drew back and stared deep into her lover's stormy grey eyes, considering the possibilities. They had all day. All weekend. The rest of their lives. She had time to learn every inch of his body, and let him learn hers. That brought a smile to her face.

"What are you thinking, my love?" he asked, running a hand across her back. "I can sense that you're thinking about me, but not the details of your thoughts."

"Good. You don't want to know the details. They're pretty sordid," she teased. She wrapped her arms around him and drew him back down into bed, but she could still see him trying to work out what she was thinking about.

"Do you wish to... make love again?" he asked tentatively

"No, not yet," she replied. "I need some time to recover. It's a little… uncomfortable in those parts right now. I just want to lie here and be happy together."

"Did I injure you in my haste last night?" he asked, his arms tightening protectively around her. "I feared that I might. I'm much larger than you."

"No, you didn't hurt me," she replied. She gave him an affectionate smile and a quick kiss. "It's just that it's new. I've never done that before. Those muscles haven't had a work-out like that before. You know how it feels when you exercise really hard, and the next morning you wake up stiff?"

"Ah." He made a sound of understanding and nodded. "Yes, I know what you mean. Then we shall just do whatever pleases you this morning, my love. Tell me what you desire."

"I desire you, Cijal," she said softly, firmly, and with great conviction. "I don't care what we do, so long as we do it together. That's all that matters to me."

Cijal smiled, and cuddled her close against him.

***

After an hour of lying together, doing nothing but swapping kisses and talking softly, Dawn's stomach began to growl. She stretched out languidly, then looked at him and suggested something that was on both of their minds. "You want some breakfast?"

"I would love some breakfast," Cijal agreed immediately. He slid out of bed and stretched as well. "I must say, human beds are very interesting to sleep in. I've never rested on anything quite so soft."

Dawn shot a curious glance at him, watching his powerful muscles ripple beneath his blue-grey skin. "Oh? What do your people sleep on?"

"Our beds are made of stone, sculpted to fit the exact contours of the sleeper's body." He glanced over his shoulder and gave her a smile. "Nereidis parents spend a great deal of time carving and re-carving to their child's bed as they grow. My father said it was something of a relief when I finally reached adulthood, so I could take on the responsibility myself."

Dawn smiled at the image that conjured up. "How sweet. Your parents must love you very much."

Cijal's expression flickered for a moment. "They do, though sometimes they have strange ways of showing it. At least, my mother does. She is very... aggressive. My father is calm and placid by contrast, but Mother can be difficult to deal with."

"No wonder you were always running off when we were kids," Dawn said. She stood up and put her robe on, then glanced at him. "Sorry, I don't think I have anything that will fit you."

"Ah, of course. One moment." Cijal vanished into the bathroom, then returned with his shorts.

"Aren't those all wet and icky?" Dawn asked, as she watched him getting dressed.

"No more than I'm used to," he replied. "This is an artificial fabric, made to be water-resistant, dirt-resistant, and quick-drying. They're a little damp now, but my body heat will dry them before we've finished eating. "

"That is interesting," she said, running a hand over the curve of his backside. "Huh, look at that. They are almost dry, even after spending the night in the shower box. They feel weird. Don't they constrict your movements?"

Cijal jumped at the unfamiliar sensation of a hand on his bottom, and shot her an amused look. "No, not really. The fabric is close-fitting, but not tight. It's designed so that I can move freely and breathe through it."

"Breathe through it?" Dawn asked, wrinkling her nose. "You breathe through your butt?"

"No!" Cijal exclaimed, laughing. "Through my skin. My people breathe through our skin when we're underwater. Or rather, our bodies absorb oxygen from the water through our skin. We use our lungs when we're out of the water, just as you do."

"Oh, I wondered about that," she admitted, then she took his hand and led him towards the kitchen. "I've wondered about so many things, and never had the chance to ask before now."

"Well, we have all day, my love," Cijal replied. "You may ask anything you please."

"Oh, I will, don't you worry," she teased. "I'll get breakfast on. In the meantime, tell me what your people eat? I've always been curious."

"We primarily eat fish," he replied, wandering over to stare out the window at the falling rain. "We also eat other things, depending on what's available. Some of my people prefer not to consume the flesh of animals, so we farm kelp and other plants. We also occasionally import exotic foods from the human realms, through one of the few groups we have regular contact with."

"So, you're omnivores, like humans?" Dawn asked. She opened the fridge, and pulled out a tray of eggs and a package of bacon.

"Officially, yes," he replied. "We can live off plant matter if we must, but we do not suffer ill health if we choose to live carnivorously, either." Cijal glanced at her and raised what passed for an eyebrow. "I once read that your people become ill if you don't eat both. Is that true?"

"Well, it's more complicated than that," Dawn explained. She set a pan on the stove, turned it on, and started cracking eggs. "We can live a vegetarian life, but you need to be careful to make sure you get all the nutrients you need. We do get really sick if we don't eat fruit or vegetables, though."

"Fascinating. My teacher told us many things about your species, but I often wondered which aspects were true and which were not." Cijal moved away from the window, wandering over to observe what she was doing. "What is this you're making?"

"Bacon and eggs," she said with a smile. "It's kind of a tradition to start your morning with bacon and eggs here. Bacon is the cured meat of an animal called a pig, and eggs are... well, it's best not to know exactly what they are, but they come from a small bird called a chicken."

"I am familiar with what eggs are in general," he said, chuckling. "Many ocean creatures lay eggs."

"Actually, that reminds me." Dawn put the lid on the frying pan, set her spatula down, then turned to face him. "I probably should have asked this earlier, but... we got so caught up in the moment last night that we didn't use any kind of protection. Do you think it's possible that you could get me pregnant?"

"I doubt it." Cijal smiled down at her, sliding his arm around her waist to draw her against his chest. "Although my people were human once, we are not anymore. I would be very surprised if we were capable of having children."

"Oh." Dawn went quiet for a moment and thought it over, then she nodded. "I think at this stage, I'm relieved. In a few years I might be sad about that, but we're too young for babies so that's okay."

"I'm glad." Cijal's expression turned playful, and his hands tightened upon her. Suddenly, Dawn found herself pressed up against the door of the refrigerator by his body. "That means we can try it again – once you recover, of course."

Before she could answer, he swooped down and kissed her. Whatever she'd planned to say was forgotten in an instant, blown away by the passion that lingered behind that kiss. It distracted them both so much that they didn't hear the sound of footsteps coming up behind them.

"Wow. You actually weren't kidding," Jessica said. Cijal spun around in an instant, protectively shoving Dawn behind him, and Jessica's brows shot up. "Whoa. Calm your tits, big guy."

"Jess!" Dawn squeaked, squeezing out from behind Cijal's bulk to forestall any danger to her friend. "I didn't think you were coming home this morning."

"I'm going back out in a second, but I had to grab a few things," Jessica said, folding her arms across her chest. "I'm going to spend the weekend at Adam's, so you two have the house to yourselves."

"Uh, that's great. Thank you." Dawn glanced back and forth between her two closest friends in the world, suddenly at a loss for what to say. "Well, um… I suppose I should introduce you. Jess, this is Cijal. Cijal, this is my best friend, Jessica. Don't worry, she already knows about you and has promised to keep your secret."

"I see." She felt Cijal relax a little, but he was still tense, and his expression was unreadable. "Greetings to you, human."

"Hey, Sea-Martian." Jessica waved, then turned on her heel and headed off towards her room. "I'm going to go get my things and get out of your hair. Have fun, kids."

Dawn cringed and shot Cijal an apologetic look. "Sorry. I needed to talk to someone, and I trust her. She's like a sister to me. Please, don't be angry with me."

Cijal gave her a long, hard stare, then drew a deep breath and nodded. "I truly hope that you made the right choice, my love."

"I did, I'm sure of it." Dawn smiled at him and squeezed his hand. "It's Jess. She wouldn't do anything to hurt me."

***

Outside, Jessica threw her overnight bag into the back seat of her car, then opened the driver's door and climbed in. She reached for her purse, pulled out her phone, and keyed in the number the man had given her when she'd first contacted him, two days prior.

As she'd discovered, the axiom that one could find anything on the Internet really was true. When she'd typed the word 'Nereidis' into a search engine, dozens of websites had come up – and any one of them would have been very interested in the information that she had to sell. The first contact called her back within minutes, and offered her a figure she couldn't resist.

She hesitated for a moment as she thought over the act that she was about to commit. Some part of her knew that it was wrong, that it was a terrible betrayal, and that she was going to lose something precious, but that was where the problem lay. Jessica didn't feel guilt. She didn't feel angry, or sad, or anything else. Occasionally she felt fear or anxiety, but that was really about it. The money was an opportunity, a chance to have a future free of those fears and anxieties. It was logical to take it.

She pressed the button to connect the call, and waited. The phone rang three times before someone picked it up, and a gruff male voice answered. "What?"

"Hey, this is Jessica Bentley," she told the person on the other end. "Is Mr Du Pont there?"

"Mr Du Pont is in a meeting at the moment."

"Oh, well, can you pass a message on to him, then?"

"What message?"

Jessica took a deep breath, then did what she felt she had to do. "Tell him that I've seen the creature we discussed, and that I know exactly where it is. If he wants the location, I expect to see the money in my bank account right away. Tell him to hurry – I don't know how long that thing is going to stay put. He has my number."

"I'm sure Mr Du Pont will be very pleased to hear that. I'll pass the message on as soon as he's available."

"Good. Thanks." Jessica hung up and put the phone back in her purse. She cast a long, thoughtful look at the house. Dawn would never forgive her, but the money was enough to give her a start in life that she'd never get slaving away at a regular job.

This Sea-Martian thing? It was an unexpected windfall, but one that she planned to take advantage of while she could. Yes, it was going to cost her the relationship she'd built with Dawn, but she could always find another best friend. Opportunities to make that kind of cash were harder to find.

A little voice in the back of her head warned her that she was making a terrible mistake, but she shook it off. In the end, the trade-off would be worth it.

Chapter 15

Dawn and Cijal spent their day together in peace, simply enjoying one another's company. The rain kept them indoors, but neither of them minded much. Once he'd recovered from his shock encounter with a strange human, Cijal resumed being his usual, affectionate self, and by mid-afternoon they were back in bed.

Once they'd finished making love again, Dawn fell into an exhausted, satisfied sleep with her head resting upon Cijal's chest. Her sleep was filled with warm, comfortable thoughts, vague and formless dreams that were pleasant enough to enjoy but not enough to remember.

Then, suddenly, her dreams were filled with earthquakes. It took a second for her mind to come awake enough to realise that someone was shaking her shoulder.

"Mm—what?" she mumbled sleepily, blinking and rubbing her eyes. It was after nightfall, and she could barely see the outline of Cijal's body in the gloom.

"There's someone else in the house," he whispered, his voice strained and urgent.

His tone brought her fully awake, though she didn't immediately share his concern. "Relax, it's probably just Jess. I'll go check. Stay here."

The bare floorboards felt so cold beneath her feet that she just wanted to crawl back into bed, but she couldn't until she'd reassured Cijal that they were safe.

With a sleepy sigh, she fumbled for her dressing gown in the dark, pulled it around her shoulders, and tied the sash.

There was a faint light shining beneath the door jamb. When she opened it, she saw Jessica silhouetted in the doorway across the hall.

"Hey," Dawn greeted her, pulling the door closed behind her. "I thought you were staying at Adam's tonight?"

Jess turned and gave her a faint smile. "Yeah, I was going to, but I had to come and tell you something."

"In the middle of the night?" Dawn asked, muffling a yawn behind one hand.

"I might not have another chance," Jess said. "I just wanted to let you know that it's not personal."

Dawn blinked owlishly, bewildered. "What?"

"This is a big opportunity for me, you know? It's a chance for me to finally get ahead in life," Jess explained. "You're not going to want to see me tomorrow, I get that. I'm just going to get my things, then I'll be out of your hair."

"Huh?" Dawn stared at her best friend in confusion. "You're leaving?"

Distracted as she was, she didn't hear the person coming up behind her until it was too late.

Suddenly, a strong arm grabbed her around the waist, pinning her arms to her sides, and a leather-clad hand clamped over her mouth. Dawn screamed and tried to bite her attacker, but the leather muffled the effectiveness of both. Although she fought as hard as she could, the man lifted her effortlessly off her feet and held her trapped.

"Don't fight it, Dee," Jess advised calmly, still standing in her bedroom doorway with her arms folded across her chest. "They want your boyfriend, not you. Just do what they tell you, and they'll let you go."

"Change of plans, kid," the black-clad man said. "Mr Du Pont wants us to grab them both."

"What?!" Jessica gasped. "But he promised he was going to leave Dawn alone!"

"Not my business, take it up with him," the man replied, his voice all professional detachment and disinterest.

Panic swelled within Dawn's chest. She fought frantically against the attacker's grasp, but her kicks were ineffective against his body armour. Worse, she suddenly realised that he was not alone. Black-clad men rushed past them, into her bedroom, and then she heard the sounds of another struggle taking place beyond her line of sight.

In a momentary burst of adrenaline, she jerked her head free and tried to scream a warning to Cijal, but all she got for her efforts was a cuffing that made her head ring. There was an electric sound, followed by a bellow that sounded more like an enraged beast than a man.

A black-clad body flew through the doorway and struck the far wall. Seconds later, Cijal charged out of the room, ripping taser darts from his chest.

Tears blurred Dawn's vision. She struggled in vain to cry out to him, but the leather-clad hand was unrelenting. Still, the muffled sound of her cries caught Cijal's attention. He turned towards her and his eyes widened. With a roar of fury, he lunged at her attacker.

The man swore and shoved her into Cijal's path, but the distraction didn't quite work as he'd anticipated. Instead of tripping over her, Cijal scooped her up and shoulder-charged the man, bowling him right out the front door. There was a terrible crash of wood splintering, then they were outside on the stoop. Cijal started forward, only to skid to a halt again when he was blinded by bright spotlights.

A second later, the sound of a dozen tasers firing at once filled the air, and Dawn screamed in pain.

***

In the black void of unconsciousness, Dawn had no concept of the passage of time – or of how lucky she'd been. She was vaguely aware that in the moment before darkness claimed her, Cijal had shielded her with his own body in an attempt to protect her. That action saved her life.

It might have been hours or even days, but eventually she began to claw her way out of the dark pit of oblivion and back to the land of the living. She shifted and tried to wipe her eyes, but her hands wouldn't respond. At first she thought that she was just having one of those dreams where she was paralysed, but eventually she came awake enough to realise that her hands were bound. With that realisation, the memories came tumbling back.

Her eyes snapped open, and she found herself in a scene right out of a horror movie. The room she was in resembled a makeshift hospital ward, except that she was completely nude and her hands were cuffed to the head of the bed. There was a strange man wearing the white apron and mask of a doctor standing at the foot of her bed, intensely focused on doing something to her most intimate parts. Dawn screamed and kicked him with all her strength.

To her surprise, she struck a solid blow; the man stumbled back and collapsed, blood staining his white mask. A moment later, the door burst open, and a pair of armed soldiers rushed in with their weapons at the ready.

Struggling to keep her terror in check, Dawn attacked them with the only weapon she had at her disposal: emotional blackmail.

"Please, please help me," she begged, very real tears welling up in her eyes. "Let me go! I haven't done anything wrong."

The men just looked at her, and then one of them barked a laugh that sent a chill right down her spine. Without a word, they grabbed the wounded doctor and carried him out of the room, leaving her alone. Tears leaked down her cheeks despite her best efforts to be brave. She tugged at the handcuffs but they were far stronger than she was. She was trapped, helpless, and worst of all she had no idea where Cijal was... or if he was even still alive.

It was cold, too. Very cold. They'd just left her shivering and naked, without anything to relieve her discomfort. There was a nasty pain in her hip from where the taser's prongs had pierced her skin, and she felt battered and bruised all over.

But, Cijal...

Dawn muffled a sob as best as she could. How could she help him if she couldn't even help herself? Her worst nightmare had come to life, and it was her own fault for trusting logic instead of her gut instinct. Cijal could be dead already, dissected on some awful scientist's table. After waiting so long to find him, the idea of losing him again was more than she could bear. She couldn't let it happen.

Dawn fought down her despair and focused on trying to get out of her restraints. The handcuffs were meant for a bigger wrist than hers, so perhaps if she were careful she might be able to slip out of them. The only problem was that she was cold and numb, and her body didn't want to respond. Every time she managed to get her hand half-way out, a tremor or a shiver ran through her and put her right back where she'd started from.

There were no windows in her whitewashed prison, so she had no way to tell if it was day or night, and no way to mark the passage of time. She guessed that about two hours passed before anyone came to look in on her, by which point she was nearly exhausted from her efforts trying to get free. She lifted her head at the sound of hinges whining, and stared at the door.

The man who entered was tall and handsome, in an arrogant sort of way. He crossed the room to stand at her bedside, his eyes hooded and his lips twisted into a distasteful sneer. Her gut churned in fear and panic, and left her feeling nauseated. Being exposed so completely in front of a stranger was a whole new kind of shame.

"I shall not beat around the bush." The creepy stranger's voice was crisp and clear, well-enunciated yet not polite. "I am Richard Du Pont. You will tell me everything you know about the Nereidis. Name your price."

"My price?" Dawn echoed.

"Yes, yes. It's always about fiduciary gain, isn't it?" Du Pont snapped, waving a hand dismissively. "Fifty thousand dollars bought your little friend's loyalty. Will that satisfy you as well?"

"She sold me out for a measly fifty grand?" Dawn gasped. Suddenly, her fear was replaced by red-hot anger. "That cow! I can't believe she'd—"

"A hundred thousand, then?" Du Pont interrupted.

"Screw you," she snarled, tugging at her restraints.

"Everyone has a price. Two hundred thousand?"

Dawn swore again and tried to kick him, but she couldn't reach. Du Pont just glared at her with barely-hidden disgust.

"Fine. A million," he snapped. "One million dollars, you tell me everything you know, and we'll let you go."

"You can go straight to hell," Dawn told him in no uncertain terms. "My loyalty has no price. I won't betray him for anything."

"Brave words, little girl," he replied. "Very well. If you will not help us willingly, then we'll use you as a pawn to break his will." Du Pont snapped his fingers and made a vague gesture towards her, then turned and left the room.

Suddenly, Dawn found herself overwhelmed by the rough hands of the soldiers. She was unshackled and lifted to her feet, then frog-marched out of the room. She tried to fight them, but they were much stronger than she was and her only reward was more pain.

"Let me go," she protested. "You can't just take me like this. I have rights. I demand to see a lawyer!"

"You can demand all you like, girl, but it won't help you," Du Pont snapped. "You seem to have forgotten that no one cares about you. It will be months before anyone even notices your disappearance, if they do at all. In the meantime, I shall do with you as I please."

"You can't do that — it's illegal!" she cried, panic swelling up in her belly all over again.

Suddenly, Du Pont spun around and grabbed her roughly by the jaw.

"I can do whatever I like, you pathetic child," he hissed through bared teeth, so close to her that she could feel his breath as he spoke. "No one will stop me. You may say you do not have a price, but you're alone in that. I'm one of the wealthiest men in the world, and money is the ultimate power. These Nereidis have something I want, and your petty moral complaints will not get in my way."

He shoved her back into the arms of her captors, then yanked open another door nearby. Inside a second makeshift ward, a couple of men in medical garb and a few guards stood around a table in the centre of the room. They parted as their leader returned, and past them Dawn could just barely see a grey-skinned body. Her heart leapt into her throat.

"Cijal?" she called, straining against the grip of the men holding her. One of them struck her and gave her a hard shake; she cried out in pain.

"Dawn?" Cijal called, his voice hoarse.

Dawn was dragged into the room and hauled back to her feet, at which point she could see Cijal strapped to a table, bound hand and foot with thick chains, another fastened around his waist. His skin was a mass of small wounds, but he didn't seem bothered by the pain, or at least not to the same degree she was.

The moment that their gazes met and he saw the injuries upon her naked body, his eyes flashed with rage. He growled something in his native language and strained against his restraints, making the whole table quiver and shake with his strength.

Du Pont smirked at them. Suddenly, he spun and struck Dawn hard across the face, then grabbed her as she fell and forced her to kneel at his feet. Cijal's answer was a bellow of pure rage, and the table groaned as he struggled to be free. Even through the dizzying haze of pain, Dawn understood the death threat from the tone of his voice, but he was just as helpless as she felt.

"So, you're fond of this little girl then, are you?" Du Pont sneered at the trapped Nereidis, and then he grabbed a handful of Dawn's hair and yanked her head back roughly. "Good. You're both very brave with your own pain, but let's see how you feel about watching one another suffer."

He held out a hand, and one of his cronies placed something in it. Dawn couldn't see what it was, but she saw a glint of steel, then felt the bite of a blade against her throat.

"No!" Cijal bellowed.

"Ah, so you do speak English after all. I thought so." Though she couldn't see his face, Dawn could hear the smirk in the man's voice. With a brutal jerk, he yanked her head back even further and flicked the tip of the knife across her cheek. She cried out in shock as the blade bit into her skin; a droplet of blood welled up, and rolled down her cheek like a tear.

"Leave her alone or I'll kill you, human," Cijal growled, murder written on his face.

"You know what I want," Du Pont growled right back, and gave Dawn another shake to punctuate his point. "Tell me where your colony is, or you can watch me take her apart, piece by piece."

"You wouldn't dare!" Dawn gasped, horrified by the very concept. "We're innocent people. Why in God's name would you do such a thing?"

"Shut up." Du Pont's voice was like ice, completely heartless and without any form of sympathy. He released her hair and struck her across the face so hard that she almost lost consciousness. "Well, creature? Is that what you want? Do you want to watch this poor girl suffer for you?"

While he was distracted, Dawn summoned the willpower to try and scramble away. There were too many guards, though — she only made it a few feet before one of them caught her by the hair again and forced her back to her knees. She swore silently to herself; for the first time in her life, she wished that she'd cut all her hair off rather than keeping it long. Instead of being a beautiful asset, now it was a painful liability.

She could hear Cijal cursing in his own tongue, and she knew what he meant even though she didn't understand the words. The sound and sight of his helplessness spurred her on and made her want to fight even harder, despite the risk of more pain. She snuck a quick glance around while the men were ignoring her, and spotted a gun strapped to the hip of the man holding her. She just had to use her head if she wanted to take advantage of the opportunity. Literally.

In a flash of adrenaline, she curled her legs beneath her and exploded upwards, head-butting the guard right in the crotch. He wasn't wearing body armour, so the breath exploded out of him and he collapsed to his knees. Dawn grabbed his weapon from its sheath and spun around, putting her back against the nearest wall.

"Let him go, right now!" she demanded, pointing the gun at Du Pont. "I swear, I will shoot you in the face!"

"You're a feisty little brat," he spat. His posture changed from aggressive to defensive, but his tone stayed derisive. "And after all that talk about being innocent? You won't pull the trigger."

"Just watch me," she growled, and then did so.

Nothing happened.

Dawn blinked in surprise, but by the time she realised the safety was still on, it was too late. Black-clad bodies bowled her over and pinned her down, and for all her feistiness she was no match for their strength.

"Don't kill her. We still need her," Du Pont ordered. "Bring her over here."

When the mound of soldiers cleared, she found her hands cuffed cruelly behind her back. She was yanked to her feet and man-handled over to Du Pont, who grabbed her roughly by the back of the neck. With no regard for her dignity or her bruised body, he propelled her forward over a nearby table.

Her face came to rest upon a warm, smooth surface. It took her concussed brain a second to realise that she was being held down with her face pressed against Cijal's stomach. She could feel him trembling beneath her cheek, but she could barely open her eyes. She was woozy and her awareness was starting to fade, but she still vaguely heard Du Pont issuing orders.

"You there, light the burner and heat this knife up. Let's start with the classics, shall we?"

It sounded like the voice was coming from the far end of a long tunnel, but she could still see the look of outrage on Cijal's handsome face.

"I-I'm sorry," she whispered haltingly. She wasn't sure if the words reached him. Tears blurred her vision and fell unrestrained onto his skin. She heard people moving around her, but she was so numb she could barely comprehend what was about to happen to her.

Cijal, on the other hand, was fully aware and could see everything they were doing.

"Stop!" he yelled suddenly.

Blearily, Dawn blinked up at him, struggling to figure out what all the yelling was about. A dark-clad figure that she vaguely recognised came into her field of vision and bent over her lover, staring at him intently.

"Did you say something, creature?" Du Pont purred, his voice taunting and repulsively arrogant.

"I said stop," Cijal repeated. "I'll cooperate, but you must cease this. I will only give you the information you want if you let her go."

"You know that's not going to happen," Du Pont replied. "She's our leverage, she's not going anywhere. But, I will guarantee that she'll remain unharmed if you give us your full cooperation. Perhaps I will let her go once you have told us everything we want to know."

"That's not good enough," Cijal told him. "You're asking me to betray my entire species. My family. All of my friends. In exchange for that, I must have your promise that you will *never* harm her in any way."

"Fine." Du Pont made a gesture towards the men holding Dawn. They released her, but she was too weak to stand on her own and slipped down to her knees. Someone caught her before she fell over completely and held her in a sitting position while she struggled to regain her strength. Her consciousness wavered, and everything sounded like it was coming from a million miles away. She vaguely heard Cijal's voice and that of their captor, but she couldn't make out what they were saying.

Sitting down helped, though. Eventually, she began to claw her way back from the edge of darkness, and things started to make sense again. She couldn't tell how much time had passed, but she could still hear the voices arguing over the terms of their agreement, so she decided that it couldn't have been that long.

Suddenly, a strange noise broke through her daze. She lifted her head, and saw the men around her looking in the direction of the sound, their expressions varying between confusion and concern.

"What is that?" Du Pont demanded. He pointed at one of his men and flicked a hand towards the door. "Go find out immediately. I shan't be interrupted!"

Several of the soldiers peeled away from the pack and hurried towards the door. The sound moved closer in bursts, punctuated by shouts and curses. Suddenly,

Dawn realised what she was hearing: gunfire. She glanced at Du Pont, and saw a deep grimace on his face. He swore at his remaining soldiers and sent two more out the door after the others.

A few seconds later, the men shouted in alarm and there was more gunfire. This time, it was right outside.

Without waiting for instruction, the final soldier ran to the door in a low crouch, his weapon at the ready. He paused in the doorway for a moment, then sprang around with his weapon raised, ready to fire.

His finger froze on the trigger.

An older gentleman in an elegantly-tailored suit stepped into her line of sight, and approached the soldier. The soldier didn't even move. He just stared at the newcomer, wide-eyed, frozen like a fly in amber.

"Dawn?" Cijal whispered, his voice low and urgent. "Dawn, are you there?"

"I'm here," she whispered back, struggling to lever herself up off the floor.

"My love, listen to me carefully." Even without seeing his face, she could hear the worry in his voice. "Whatever may happen, do not make eye-contact with that man."

She started to say something, but the man in the suit was moving again. There was no time to think or ask questions.

"Sleep," the well-dressed man said; a moment later, the soldier collapsed like a sack of potatoes. Then, the gentleman turned towards their captor and gave him a long, hard look. "Richard Maximillian Du Pont. Your mother warned me to keep an eye on you."

"You!" Du Pont spat, making no attempt to hide his rage. "Get out of my house, Logan. How dare you come in here and murder my men?"

177

"Murder? No one's been murdered." Logan's lips twisted into an amused smirk, and then his bright blue eyes shifted towards Dawn and Cijal. "It seems that Carienne was quite correct, though. You are a very troubled young man."

"Leave my house immediately! This is none of your business!" Du Pont's voice rose to an undignified yell. Over his shouting, Dawn faintly heard the sound of a gun being drawn – then, suddenly, she was yanked back to her feet. The movement was so unexpected that she didn't have time to fight back. The next thing she knew, there was an arm around her throat and a gun against her temple. "How dare you come here after what you did to my mother? Get out of my house, or I'll kill this girl. Do you want that, Logan? More blood on your hands?"

"A hostage, Richard? Really?" Logan said, his voice thick with condescension. "Your mother killed *herself*. It was her choice. There was no conspiracy. Now, put that gun down and let the girl go."

Dawn squeezed her eyes closed, half to protect herself from whatever the mysterious man in the suit was going to do, and half out of fear of seeing her own brain-matter smeared on the wall in the last few seconds before death – but Du Pont didn't pull the trigger. To her surprise, he lowered the gun and released her. She pulled away the moment that she could, and Du Pont made no attempt to stop her. He just stood there, looking dazed and confused.

"That's a good boy," Logan said. With a strange, sinuous grace, he stepped forward and held out his hand. "Now, give me the keys to the restraints."

Dawn stared at them sideways, careful not to look the older man in the eye. She heard footsteps out in the hall, then more men appeared in the doorway. They were not the same soldiers she'd seen before, not even close. These men were dressed to the nines in slick designer suits, well-groomed, and looked as relaxed as if they were out taking an evening stroll. Not one of them was armed. Several of them shot her appraising looks, glances that left her feeling self-conscious.

"Dawn," Cijal whispered again. Nervous about the strange men, she backed away to the side of her lover's bed and looked down at him. He gave her a faint, reassuring smile even though he couldn't move. "Don't make eye-contact with any of them, either."

She nodded quietly, and shot a quick glance over her shoulder, careful not to meet their gazes. "Who are they?"

"Friends." The answer didn't come from Cijal, but from the man named Logan. "William Logan, Cornelius Pharmaceuticals. A pleasure to meet you both, in spite of the circumstances. Demetri, go find the young lady something to wear, would you?"

Logan unlocked her cuffs, and one of the other men wrapped a white lab coat around her. Cijal was freed a moment later, and the first thing he did was hug her so tight that for a second she couldn't breathe. A moment later, relief took her breath away a second time. Somehow, some way, they were safe – or at least, safer. Whoever the strange men were, they didn't seem interested in harming them. That was all that mattered.

"Well, this is interesting," Logan commented. "I was going to ask how a Nereidis managed to get himself captured, but I think the answer to that question has just made itself quite obvious. Does your family know you have a mortal companion, son?"

Cijal grunted softly, a sound that might have been a laugh or merely an acknowledgement of the truth. "Of course not, but I do not care. Her approval and her love are the only things that matter."

"Very, very interesting," Logan said, staring at the two of them thoughtfully. "Your people are the most reclusive of us. They're not going to be pleased if you show up with a mortal in tow. They may even kill her."

"I know," Cijal said softly. "I never intended for this to happen. I thought no one knew about me except for her, and I trust her."

"It's my fault," Dawn said. "I told my best friend about him. I thought I could trust her, but I was wrong. I'm sorry, Cijal." Tears welled up in her eyes. She buried her face in his chest to hide them. "I'm so, so sorry."

Cijal went silent for a long moment, and then he hugged her tight and kissed the top of her head. "I forgive you, my love. I suspected you would talk to someone, and yet I came anyway. It is not your fault."

"Well, let's get you two out of here, and we'll decide what to do with you once you're safe," Logan said. He turned and gestured to one of his men. "Gentlemen, you know what to do."

The men nodded and fanned out to do whatever it was that they apparently knew to do. Cijal and Dawn both looked curiously at Logan.

"Young Richard here is the son of one of my late associates," Logan explained, gesturing at Du Pont, who still stood staring into space as though hypnotised. "He's been on our radar for some time due to his increasingly rash actions. Capturing and torturing a Nereidis is a step too far. My men will recondition him and his soldiers, so they'll remember nothing of this – and never do anything like it in future."

"Good." Cijal's voice came out as a low growl, and Dawn felt his big body tense up. Sensing his anger, she leaned up on tiptoes to kiss his cheek.

"Let's just go, Cijal. I want to go home," she said, to deter him from doing anything he might regret later. "Or somewhere safe, at least. It doesn't matter where, so long as we're together."

Cijal looked at her, and the anger filtered out of his expression, replaced by concern. He nodded once and gave her a hug, then shot a glance at William Logan. "Can you take us back to my people?"

"I can," he said simply, then turned and left the room. Without asking permission, Cijal swept Dawn up in his arms and hurried after the mysterious stranger.

Chapter 16

The steady throb of the helicopter's rotors drowned out any hope of conversation, so Dawn sat quietly and just waited for them to get to wherever they were going. Opposite them, William Logan and a pair of his associates sat, working away diligently on their smartphones. At least, she assumed they were working. For all she knew, they were having an Angry Birds marathon.

She didn't really care whether they were working or playing, though. Once the adrenaline had drained out of her system, it left her feeling dizzy, nauseated, and aching all over from her impressive collection of bruises. Before they'd boarded the helicopter, Logan's associates had brought them both food, water, and clothing, then a medic had checked them over and given her pain killers. The painkillers had helped for a while, but they were starting to wear off. She wished she'd asked for more.

Beside her, Cijal looked strange dressed in a pair of jeans, but they were the only clothing they'd been able to find that fit him on such short notice. Dawn thoughtfully ran her nails over the fabric, which drew a curious look from him. He tried to say something, but she just shook her head and smiled at him; she couldn't hear him over the noise and the pounding in her head. He nodded understandingly, and put one big arm around her shoulders to pull her up against his side.

Dawn closed her eyes and tried to rest, but the noise made her head throb. She wanted to ask how much further they'd have to travel, but there was no point in trying with the noise. Besides, it couldn't be that far. They'd been traveling over water for more than ten minutes.

Just as she was thinking that, she felt the helicopter's forward motion ease to a halt. She glanced out the window, and saw a tiny silver pod glinting in the water below them, gradually getting bigger as the helicopter lost altitude. She shot a nervous glance at Cijal, but he just smiled.

When the helicopter was low enough to almost touch the water, Logan got up and opened the side door, letting in a blast of ocean-scented wind. With complete disregard for the risk to their fine suits, the three men flicked a rope ladder out the door and climbed down one by one, leaving Cijal and Dawn to last.

Never a fan of heights, Dawn clung to Cijal's arm as he guided her to the edge. He showed no such concern. With gentle hands, he helped her onto the ladder and shielded her with his own body as they climbed down, so there was no way she could fall without being caught.

Eventually, all of them reached the shining pod. It slid open to reveal a small cockpit, manned by a pair of grey-skinned pilots. Once they were inside, the roof of the pod slid closed and sealed with a soft hiss. She looked around as she was guided to a seat, surprised by the level of technology around her.

"For some reason, I pictured your people as kind of medieval," she admitted to Cijal. "I mean, you've mentioned your technology before, but this is like something out of a science fiction movie. Cool."

"This is but one of the many things I never thought I'd have the chance to show you," he replied, giving her hand a soft squeeze as they settled side-by-side in the passenger's compartment, with William Logan and his associates behind them. Cijal gave her a grin, then called something to the Nereidis pilots in his own language.

One of them glanced back at them and rolled his eyes. He touched a couple of buttons on the dashboard in front of him, and the entire canopy of the vehicle suddenly turned translucent. Cijal reached up and rapped his knuckles on the canopy, to show her that it was still solid, but despite that knowledge she still gasped when the vehicle took off. Bubbles surrounded them for a few seconds as the pod broke the surface, and when they cleared she discovered that she could see everything. Fish swam lazily in schools all around them, hardly bothered by the streamlined, elliptical shape of the little vessel. Her fear swiftly gave way to delight; the view was unlike anything she'd ever experienced.

"I wish I had a camera," she said to Cijal. "Or maybe my paints. This is amazing. How did it do that?"

Cijal laughed and hugged her. "You've never once asked how I do the same thing with my own body, but you ask about the pod?"

"Well, I just assumed that was a biological thing," she replied, laughing right along with him. "I thought it'd be rude to ask."

"It's not rude, my love," he told her. "I'm happy to answer any of your questions, when I can. In this case, though, I don't know the answer. I am not an engineer. My training as a Watcher primarily includes combat, tracking, and stealth."

"And English," she reminded him with a playful nudge.

"And English," he agreed. "I can ask the pilots for you, if you really want to know."

"Nah, it's okay. I don't want to know that much." She grinned at him. One of the men behind her snorted a laugh. She glanced back at them, then gave them a shy smile. "I really do want to know who you guys are, though. You look like the men in black."

"Unfortunately, you are not cleared to know exactly who we are," William Logan answered dryly. "But I can tell you that I'm a lawyer. Does that answer your question?"

"A lawyer?" Dawn echoed. "No, that doesn't really explain anything. I've never seen a lawyer do what you did."

Logan chuckled and nodded. "Indeed. Let's just say that whapping young Master Du Pont on the nose with a rolled-up subpoena like a disobedient mongrel is not the limit of our abilities and leave it at that, shall we?"

He went silent after that and looked away; his body language told her that the conversation was over. Dawn took the hint. After what she'd seen them do, she didn't really want to antagonise them.

***

The water began to darken as the pod dove deeper, skimming along the edge of an underwater cliff, then it took a sudden turn and they plunged into shadow. For a moment, Dawn worried they were going to hit the cliff face, but they didn't. Instead, a section of the cliff slid away in a cloud of bubbles, to reveal a narrow passageway beyond.

She clung to Cijal's hand while the pod sped along the tunnel, which was barely wide enough for the pod to fit through. Suddenly, the pod changed directions and shot upwards again, breaking the surface in a glistening wave of effervescence. Dawn gasped in surprise, her eyes widening at the sight that unfolded before her.

She'd been expecting a small town with little huts and a handful of people, but that was not what greeted her at all. The pod came up in a huge, open area that resembled nothing so much as a harbour, hollowed out in the heart of a mountain. Instead of open sky, a massive, intricately carved dome of stone covered the entire cityscape – and it was a true city, not a town.

A hundred pods in a variety of sizes flanked the edge of the harbour. Beyond them, she saw buildings and people that vaguely resembled the familiar aspects of human life, but the differences made them even more alien. As the pod moved closer to the city, she realised that everything was glistening, but it wasn't the shine of water – the buildings themselves were made of some kind of limestone, polished by Nereidis hands until it shone. The city was lit artificially by a thousand tiny, sparkling lights, which lit the cavern as bright as day, but with a bluish cast that made the stone resemble the water outside.

"How beautiful," Dawn murmured. Cijal's only answer was a soft grunt. She glanced at him and saw a strange expression on his face, a look of grim intensity that set her on edge. "What is it?"

"My parents," he said softly, pointing towards a small group waiting on the docks. "And my brother, his wife, and the high elder, as well. This is going to be... unpleasant."

Dawn stared at him for a moment, then turned and looked at the group. It only took her a moment to identify the towering figures of his father and brother, but at a distance she couldn't tell which was which. They both appeared young and fit, and of a like age.

The females were no easier to figure out. They were much smaller than the males, and none of them looked old enough to have a nineteen year old son, let alone be called an elder.

"I don't know which one is which," she admitted.

Cijal smiled, though the smile didn't drive the concern from his eyes. "Look at the necklaces. The female with the most necklaces is our high elder. She is rumoured to be one of the First Ones, those who were once human, long ago. If true, that would make her more than ten thousand years old. My mother and father are the ones standing beside her. Their names are Nasara and Eiran. My older brother, Lauros, is standing behind them, and the female beside him is Beai, his wife."

Hearing their names made her heart leap up into her throat. "Am I supposed to call them by name? Oh God, do they even speak English?"

"Beai does not, but the others do," Cijal said, hugging her gently to try and reassure her. "My father and brother are both Watchers, my mother is a linguist, and the High Elder handles most of our affairs with the outside world. As for whether you should talk to them..." Cijal hesitated, then he shrugged. "If they ask you questions, you should answer. Otherwise, it might be best for you to let me speak to them first."

"I am absolutely fine with that," Dawn replied dryly.

There was a soft clunk as the pod eased into a berth, then the lid hissed back and let in a burst of salty air. Cijal rose to his feet and fell into line behind William Logan and his men, leaving her the last to climb the ramp back onto dry land. She followed quietly in Cijal's footsteps, taking care to stay small and mostly out of sight.

"My lady, it has been far too long," William Logan said, approaching the Nereidis elder with a hand extended. The two shook, though the Nereidis seemed slightly uncomfortable with the gesture.

"Indeed it has, Elder," she replied, her English tinged by the same sort of curious accent as Cijal's. "I thank the Cabal for freeing our young one from captivity."

"Of course," Logan replied. He bowed, and gestured for Cijal to come forward. "It is in all our best interests that your people remain hidden for the time being. You'll be glad to know that we arrived in time to prevent him from coming to harm."

"Good," she said, then she looked at Cijal as he came forward. "And what have you to say for yourself, young Watcher? How did you become caught?"

Cijal bowed his head, a gesture that was respectful but showed no sign of guilt or remorse. "I was on the land, Elder. Willingly. The humans took me by surprise."

The High Elder's hairless brows rose sharply. "You know very well that you are forbidden from going to the land, as are we all. Why would you disobey?"

He hesitated for a long second, then shot a glance over his shoulder at Dawn. "Elder, I was visiting with my Chosen One."

"What?" she gasped, her eyes widening.

"You've been courting a human?" Nasara cried. "You told me you were courting a girl in another colony! You lied to me!"

"I did," Cijal said, his voice tense. "I knew you would disapprove, Mother. You've made it clear that you hate the humans, but that is your choice, not mine. I am old enough to make my own choices, and I have chosen. I love Dawn and she has accepted my trinket."

Before either of them could react, Nasara stormed past her gathered family and shoved Cijal aside, to stare at Dawn with open hostility.

"I see no trinket around her throat," she growled.

Suddenly afraid for her safety, Dawn took a step backwards, but Cijal swiftly put himself between her and his angry mother.

"The trinket was lost during our captivity, but I will make her another," he told her, drawing himself up to his full height. "I will not allow you to harm her, Mother. I will defend her if I must. Do not force me to do so."

Dawn stared back and forth between the grey-skinned bodies, feeling completely out of place and more than a little frightened. She could sense a growing tension amongst the Nereidis but she didn't fully understand the cause. Still, even she could see that Cijal's mother was furious, and none of the others looked particularly happy either.

"You will not bring a land-walker into our home," Nasara snarled, making a sharp gesture. "I forbid it."

"I must also forbid this," the High Elder cut in, shaking her head. "Cijal, you know better than this. We cannot have a human here. It is not appropriate." She looked at William Logan and bowed her head. "We appreciate you returning our son to us. Please take this human female back with you when you leave, and ensure that she cannot speak of this to anyone."

Logan opened his mouth to say something, but Cijal cut him off.

"No!" he cried, his hands clenching into fists at his side. "If Dawn is not welcome here, then neither am I. I have loved her my entire life, and I will not be parted from my Chosen One just because you insist on perpetuating the xenophobic ways of our ancestors!"

"And where would you go, child?" the High Elder asked. "You have already seen what the land-walkers will do to you. If you choose to follow her back to the land, then it will almost certainly happen again. Would you die for this human?"

"In a heartbeat, Elder One," Cijal replied. "Allow me but a moment to gather my possessions and farewell my family, and then we will be gone."

"If I may speak a moment?" William Logan said, his voice smooth and even in the midst of so much anger. The Nereidis all looked at him, and their elder nodded her consent. He looked at Cijal, his expression stern but not unfriendly. "You know she's mortal. You'll have her for sixty or seventy years, and then she'll die. How thoroughly have you thought this through? Are you really willing to give up your entire life here for a few decades out of all eternity?"

"I have thought of nothing but this for a long time," Cijal snapped back, looking irritated by the lawyer's tone. "I know she's mortal. I don't care. I would rather have her for seventy years than never have her at all. You say that I would be giving up my life, but that's not true. She is my life."

"In that case, I might be able to help," Logan replied, then he looked back at the group of Nereidis. "Release the boy into the care of the Cabal. I have a use for him, and I can ensure his safety."

"Elaborate," the High Elder said.

"I recently lost a son to my enemies under similar circumstances, and I must admit that I have many regrets over that matter," Logan replied. "My clan owns an island in the tropics. It's off-limits to all mortals except those who serve us. We're building a resort on the island, aimed at an immortal clientele base, and we're going to need staff."

"You would take us both?" Cijal asked. "You will not try to separate us?"

"So long as you don't betray us to our enemies or set things on fire," Logan said, with a playful smirk. "Perhaps if the two of you prove adequately useful, we may even consent to allow her to have the elixir one day."

Dawn had no idea what they were talking about, but Cijal's eyes lit up.

"Then I would certainly be willing," he said. He turned and looked at Dawn, his eyebrows raised. "Your vote is just as important as mine, my love. What do you think?"

"I think there are worse fates than living out my life on a tropical island with the man of my dreams, even if I do have to work for it," Dawn replied, then she gave Logan a shy smile. "I agree, too."

"Good, good," Logan said, nodding. "And you, my lady High Elder? How do you feel about this compromise? You can consider it an act of good faith, on behalf of our future relations."

"Having an ambassador amongst your Cabal does seem like a good idea," the High Elder said thoughtfully. "As you wish. If you will ensure the human's silence and take responsibility for Cijal's future, then I offer my consent as well."

"You cannot be serious!" Nasara cried, her voice as sharp as a knife. "You're encouraging my son to mate with a land-walker? Just look at her! The entire idea is ludicrous and disgusting!"

"Nasara, stop," Eiran said, his deep, powerful voice cutting through the argument. He strode forward and caught his wife by the shoulders, turning her to face him. "This is Cijal's choice to make, not ours. Your mother disapproved of our union as well, and yet we are happy together, are we not? Isn't your son's happiness the most important thing? If he finds joy with a human, then so be it. It is as the Fates will it."

"But—" she started to protest, but he cut her off.

"No buts," he said, his tone gentle despite its power. "He's an adult. As you pointed out, they can't stay here." Eiran smiled sadly, cupping her cheek in the palm of one big hand. "Choose your words now with care. We're going to lose our son today, one way or another. Do not lose his love as well, or you will regret it forever."

"I-I—" Nasara froze for a long moment, staring up at him. Suddenly, her eyes filled with tears and her shoulders slumped. "You're right. I just... I don't want to lose my child."

"I'm not a child anymore, Mother," Cijal said softly, his deep voice a mirror of his father's. "I'm old enough to make my own choices. I choose Dawn. She's a good person, and she makes me happy. I would like you to get to know her, if you're willing to open your mind, and your heart. We have a few minutes to speak while I gather my things – assuming the High Elder will allow it?"

"I will," the High Elder replied. "Take your time, young one. You've chosen a difficult path, but one that I hope ultimately prove rewarding. Go with your family; I'll work out the details of your arrangement with the Cabal."

Cijal nodded. He turned back to Dawn, and offered his hand to her. "Come, my love; there are many things I want to show you, and people I want you to meet before we leave."

"Okay," Dawn agreed willingly. She accepted the offered hand, and followed him deeper into the ethereal underwater city.

As they walked, she felt two powerful emotions clench her stomach: hope and joy.

***

A few hours later, they were in the helicopter on their way back to land. Cijal had all his belongings packed into a smooth plastic case, which sat on the seat beside him. Dawn sat on the other side, leaning against him, her fingers comfortably entwined through his.

At Logan's suggestion, they were on their way back to the house on the beach. She had to get her own things, after all – and then there was the matter of what to do about Jessica. Once she'd explained what happened, Logan had agreed that Jessica could not be left unattended to spread their secrets.

Over the sound of the helicopter's rotors, Dawn faintly heard the sound of Logan's phone ringing. He pulled it out of his pocket and answered it.

"Logan speaking." There was a pause, and then he issued a soft grunt and nodded. "Good. We're about five minutes away. Make sure she doesn't leave."

"They found her?" Dawn asked.

William Logan nodded and gave her a wry smile. "She's still at the property. Not the cleverest Judas I've ever dealt with, I must say."

"If she were clever, then she wouldn't have sold her best friend out for money," Dawn answered bitterly. "I was the only person in the whole world who loved her like family. I still can't believe that she did that."

"Some people have a streak of evil in them that runs all the way to the core," Logan replied. "Others just see an opportunity and take it, without thinking about the consequences"

Dawn looked at him, sensing the pain hidden beneath his words. "Is that what your son did?"

"No." Logan sighed heavily and shook his head. "My son... did much the same thing as young Cijal is doing now. He had everything – money, power, prestige – and he threw it all away for the sake of love."

"I'm sorry," Dawn said sympathetically. "At least he's happy, right?"

"Yes. There is that," Logan said. "Still, I wish he'd let us find him happiness here instead."

"Sometimes you just have to let people choose their own path, or they'll never truly be happy," Dawn said. She closed her eyes and rested her head against Cijal's shoulder, letting his warmth comfort her. He hugged her, resting his cheek against her temple in return. The group fell silent for the last few minutes, until the helicopter began to descend.

"Now, there is the matter of your former friend's memories," Logan said suddenly, his voice carrying a note of darkness that made Dawn sit up and take notice. "My people not only have the ability to erase memories completely, but to replace them with whatever we see fit. It seems appropriate to let you have some input into your betrayer's punishment."

"Oh." Dawn stared at him, turning the concept over in her mind. As she did, she thought back over Jessica's betrayal, and anger began to bubble up in her mind again. If Logan hadn't already been watching Du Pont's estates, then both she and Cijal might have been dead — or worse.

"And there is the money, as well," Logan added, his eyes twinkling with interest as he watched her. "I feel we would be perfectly justified taking that away from her. You won't need money where you're going, but you can have it if you wish."

Her anger burst, replaced by a sudden moment of clarity.

"No. Let her keep it. I don't care about the money, but she does," she said. "As long as I've known her, Jessica's been anxious about money. Something to do with her parents, I think. I don't know. I think... I think there something wrong with her, inside. I don't want to hurt her, I want to help her. Can we do that?"

"You are a very interesting young lady," Logan said, smiling at her. "I think I'm going to like you, Miss Fitzpatrick. Yes, we can help her. Anything else?"

Dawn thought about it for a second, and then she nodded slowly. "Yes. I don't want her to become a different person, just a healthy person. Can you please make sure she doesn't forget her parents or the guy she's been dating? I don't think the thing with Adam will last long, but I still want to give it a chance. You never know, maybe he's her soulmate. Oh, and above all, please make sure that she doesn't lose her love of music and the guitar - think that might be the only thing she really *does* love, and I'd hate to take it away from her."

"We can certainly do that," Logan agreed. "If you wish, we can give her musical talents a little boost and place her in employment, so we can keep an eye on her."

"It's starting to sound like we're rewarding her for betraying me," Dawn said dryly, but she nodded anyway. "Do it. Give her the chance at a successful life that fate never did. Let's see what she does with a second chance."

"Well, this is going to be quite fascinating," Logan said, his smile widening. "Would you like the chance to talk to her before I let my boys have at her?"

"Yes, yes I would," Dawn said. Unlike Logan, there was no smile on her face.

***

Jessica whistled to herself as she wandered around the house, packing her belongings into her backpack and the suitcase she'd taken from Dawn's room. Every so often, she stopped walking and looked over at her guitar, then shook her head and forced herself to keep going.

"No regrets," she muttered to herself. "No regrets..."

Jessica closed the suitcase and went over to grab her packet of cigarettes off the dresser. She put one to her lips and was about to light up when a voice behind her almost made her jump out of her skin.

"None at all?"

Jessica spun around, the packet of cigarettes falling from her hand and tumbling to the ground. In the doorway, a familiar figure stood quietly, watching her.

"Dawn!" she gasped. "You got away?"

"Yeah, I got away," Dawn said softly, her voice carrying no trace of anger or vengefulness. "When I first came here, I came looking for closure. I'm back again for the same reason. Closure. I lost my real family years ago, but now I've lost my foster sister as well. I need to know why."

Jessica shrugged, bending down to pick her lighter up off the floor. "It was a lot of money. I need money."

"More than you needed me?" Dawn asked.

"It wasn't supposed to go down like that," Jessica replied, grimacing and shaking her head. "They were just supposed to grab him. It wasn't... ugh, like I've been trying to teach you since forever, Dee – you can't trust anyone in this messed-up world. Not even me."

"That's not true, Jess," Dawn told her gently. "There are plenty of people, good, honest people, people that deserve to be trusted."

Just at that moment, several dark-suited men appeared through the doorway. Jessica took another step back, eyeing them warily.

"Don't worry," Dawn said. "They're not going to hurt you. They're going to help you. They're going to make you feel better. I'm going away now and we'll never see each other again, but I'll always remember you and always love you, Jess — even when you don't remember me anymore."

She gave her former best friend one last sad smile, then left the room. The men in suits filed in to replace her, then the last one through closed the door quietly behind him.

Dawn took a deep breath and shut her eyes, fighting the wave of grief that rose up inside her. Even though she trusted that Logan's men were going to help Jessica, she still felt like she'd lost something precious, a huge part of her life that was now gone forever. While she was recovering, Logan came over and put a reassuring hand on her shoulder.

"I see there's some damage from Du Pont's men," he said. "I'll arrange for my staff to repair everything, and remove any trace of the attack."

"Thank you," Dawn said, giving him a weak smile. "This isn't my house, so I appreciate it. My parents owned it when I was a child, but it was sold when they died and I can't afford to buy it back."

Logan hesitated for a moment, a thoughtful look flickering across his face. "The Cabal is always in need of real estate in discreet locations. I'll purchase the property. I'm sure we'll find a use for it, and that way it'll still be in the family."

"The family?" Dawn stared at him, curious and nervous at the same time. "Does this mean that you're actually going to tell me who you are now?"

"Well, I suppose there's no harm, now that you're one of ours," Logan said with a shrug. "You've already heard our name: we're the Cabal. We are ancient, powerful, and possess abilities not unlike your young friend, Cijal. Unlike the Nereidis, we're much closer to our human roots. The Cabal are like an extended family, bound together by ancient traditions and a like-minded way of looking at the world. You'll learn more about us later, but the important thing to know is that we take care of those who are loyal to our family."

The thought brought a smile to her face. "I'm not sure about the ancient, super-human immortals thing, but having a family does sound nice. I miss that." She paused for a moment, then glanced towards her room. "I know the real estate agent who has the house for sale. If you'd like, I can call her right now."

"That would expedite the process," Logan replied. "Please do."

"Okay. I'll just be a minute," Dawn said, then she went off to find her phone and Marilyn Ascott's card. Both were exactly where she'd left them. She keyed in the number, and held the phone up to her ear while it rang.

A few seconds later, Marilyn's voice answered. "Hello?"

"Hi, Mrs Ascott. It's Dawn. Dawn Fitzpatrick," she said. "Sorry to bother you."

"Oh, hello dear! It's never a bother. How are you?"

"I'm..." The question forced her to hesitate and think it over. How was she? "I've had a long day. Some really strange things have happened, but... the short story is that I've found some family members I didn't know existed. I'm going to be going away for a while, and I wanted to say goodbye – and thank you."

"Oh! That's wonderful, dear," Mrs Ascott exclaimed. "You of all people deserve to find happiness. We'll miss you, of course, but you're welcome back any time."

"Thank you." Dawn paused for a moment to swallow the emotions that rose up in her throat and to take a deep breath. "I appreciate that. I really do. But, there's something else. I found someone who wants to purchase the house. Can I put him on?"

"Of course! That's my job, after all."

Dawn chuckled softly at the joke. "Okay. Bye, Mrs Ascott. Thank you for being so kind to me."

She handed the phone to Logan, who took it from her and put it to his ear. "Good afternoon, my name is William Logan. As Miss Fitzpatrick said, I'm interested in purchasing the house."

There was a pause, then Logan nodded to himself. "Yes, that price will be fine. I'll have my people contact your people. You'll have the funds by the end of the week. Excellent. I see Miss Fitzpatrick has your card, so I'll take care of everything. Have a pleasant day." He ended the call, and handed the phone back to Dawn. "Done."

"Done?" Dawn echoed. "Just like that?"

"Just like that." Logan smiled at her and gave her a wink. "One thing you'll come to learn about the Cabal is that we have a great deal of power. And speaking of power, I may be able to give you a better answer to the question of 'why' than your former friend was able to, if you want to know."

Dawn stared at him, surprised. "What do you mean?"

"My people have gifts of the mind, and I've been honing my skills for a very long time," Logan said, tapping the side of his head. "It's up to you if you want to know though."

"I..." Dawn hesitated, then she shrugged. "I don't know. Will it change anything?"

"Yes and no," Logan said, his expression turning serious. "It will at least reassure you that you made the right choice. My men are inside her head as we speak. She's suffered quite a bit of psychological damage."

"I suspected as much," Dawn said with a heavy sigh. "What's wrong with her? Is it my fault?"

"I don't think so." Logan shook his head thoughtfully, staring in the direction of the closed door to Jessica's bedroom. "She isn't angry at you. She doesn't hate you. She's almost completely disconnected from her feelings. There are a few conditions that could cause emotional disassociation, mostly related to some kind of trauma."

"Her parents," Dawn concluded. "She watched her mother die a long, drawn-out, painful death, and then her father committed suicide. She always refused to go to grief counselling. She kept saying that she was fine. I guess she wasn't fine after all."

"She's about as far from fine as one person can be," Logan agreed. "My men are mending the damage. When they're done, she'll be the person she was meant to be instead of the one that circumstances forced her to become."

Dawn let out a heavy sigh and nodded. "Good – and thank you. That does make me feel better."

"I know," Logan said, placing a fatherly hand on her shoulder. "Go fetch your belongings. I'll keep an eye on things here."

Dawn nodded, and headed into her bedroom. She discovered that her suitcase was gone and the contents had been dumped all over the floor. She muttered something unladylike beneath her breath, and knelt down to pick up her shoes.

The sound of her voice drew Cijal out of the bathroom. His shadow fell across her before she realised that he was there, but when she looked up she saw a smile on his face. It took a second before she realised that he had his necklaces back on, which she hadn't seen since before his captivity.

"Hey, you found your trinkets," she said. "I couldn't remember if you took them off before bed or not. I'm glad they're still here. I know how much they mean to you."

"They do, and I found something else that might please you," Cijal said, his smile broadening. He opened his hand to reveal a tiny crystal crab nestled upon his palm. "I spotted this in the bushes beside the door while you were busy talking to the humans. It appears that the clasp broke during the struggle, and it fell off."

"Oh!" Surprised and delighted, Dawn took the little crab and clutched it to her heart. "Thank you, Cijal. This means the world to me."

Cijal leaned down to touch her chin, guiding it up into a gentle kiss. When they parted, he ran his hand along the curve of her jaw. "Good. I created it for you to show you how much I love you. And I do. Let us never be parted again."

Dawn just smiled, and leaned up to kiss him again.

Epilogue

"Hold still, please," Dawn instructed, struggling not to laugh. Of all the people that she'd painted since joining the Cabal, it was always the younger immortals who squirmed the most.

"Will this take much longer?" the woman complained anxiously, looking at her watch. "I'm going to be late for a meeting."

"How about I take your photograph and paint from that?" she suggested, setting her brush down. "It won't be quite as realistic, but at least you can come and pick it up later."

The young immortal nodded, her relief quite obvious. Dawn fetched her Polaroid camera from a shelf nearby, and the young woman struck a pose long enough for Dawn to take her picture, then she was gone before the picture even finished developing.

Dawn chuckled to herself as she stuck the picture to her reference board, beside the familiar snapshots of her family.

"Kids these days," she said to no one in particular. "No patience at all."

"That sounds like someone I know," a voice said, as familiar as the photographs she'd carried half way around the world. Cijal walked in off the porch a moment later, and came over to inspect her work. "Not bad."

"I swear, they've got all the time in the world but will they sit still for an hour so I can do their portrait? No, never." Dawn laughed merrily, leaning up on tiptoes to plant a kiss on his cheek.

In the five years since that fateful day deep beneath the ocean, she'd never felt a moment of regret over her choice. The Cabal's resort was a glorious place, set on an island in the Caribbean that was surrounded by the most magnificent turquoise water she'd ever seen.

For the first year or so, she'd earned her keep as a cook and a barista, but the beautiful surroundings had inspired her so much that she'd spent all her free time with a brush in hand. One of her Immortelle managers eventually noticed her talent, and then suddenly she found herself working mostly as an artist. As she soon discovered, the Cabal were great patrons of the arts and appreciated her skill with a brush far more than her mediocre cooking ability.

Cijal, on the other hand, had gone straight back to the place he knew best as soon as they'd arrived: the ocean. The Cabal had tasked him with keeping the waters directly around the island clean and safe. It was a task he excelled at; he was a protective man by nature, and enjoyed taking care of the things that mattered to him most.

Once the resort actually opened, he'd found himself in a slightly more unusual position. He became an object of fascination to the members of the Cabal and their guests, and was often called upon to give talks about his people and their place in the great scheme of things.

"Well, I'm glad she's gone," Cijal said, wrapping his arms around her, "because you seem to have forgotten our lunch date."

"Is it lunch time already?" Dawn gasped in surprise and squirmed around, trying to get a look at the clock.

He distracted her with a kiss, then gave her a gentle squeeze and released her back onto her own feet. "It is, and I have something important I want to discuss with you."

"Oh?" she said. "Is it serious? Should I be afraid?"

"Oh yes," he replied playfully. "Be very afraid."

"You're breaking up with me, aren't you?" she joked, and Cijal laughed.

"Hardly. Quite the opposite, in fact." With one hand on the small of her back, he drew her up against him and gazed down at her adoringly. "I think that we've courted long enough. I want you to become my wife, but I don't know the proper human traditions."

"Human traditions are boring," Dawn answered, trying to hide the flush of pleasure that rose in her cheeks beneath a veil of playful humour. "I'd love to marry you, though. Let's do it whatever way is traditional for your people."

"Hmm. As you wish." Cijal stared down at her thoughtfully, his eyes falling half-closed. "We have quite complex ceremonies, and we would need an elder. Let me look into it."

"Whatever we need to do, I'm sure they'll let us hold the ceremony here," she said. "You know how the Cabal are. Any excuse for a party."

Cijal grinned and nodded at her. "There is nothing wrong with a good party."

"Careful, you're starting to sound like one of them," she teased, then she squirmed out of his embrace and grabbed his hand instead. "Come on, let's go get some lunch. We've got a lot of work ahead of us."

"Work?" Cijal echoed. "Marrying me is work?"

"No, marrying you is fun, but getting married is work," she replied. "That's what the honeymoon is for, after all – to relax after the stress of getting married."

"Ah, I see," Cijal said. "You realise, of course, that my mother would kill us both if we didn't invite her to the wedding?"

"Don't worry, we'll figure something out," she replied. "We got on just fine when she visited last winter. I think we're finally coming to terms with one another."

"And a great relief that is," Cijal commented. Dawn laughed and dragged him out of the room, and her buoyancy left him smiling.

In the last five years, he and Dawn had found a degree of happiness together that he'd never dared to dream about. Now, she was to be his wife. The only thing left to do was to figure out some way to keep her at his side for the rest of his eternity, and that was just a matter of time.

The Immortality Clause

CLAUDIA BELL #1

For as long as Claudia Bell could remember, she'd known that there was something very wrong with our world. There were too many inconsistencies – the facts just didn't add up. As a young law graduate, she saw her new job at Cornelius Pharmaceuticals not just as an opportunity to develop her career, but also as a means to find the truth. Driven by a need to discover more about the shadowy, undying Immortelle and the truth about her own family, she crosses the Tasman and takes a step into the unknown.

What she finds is not what she expected. Thrown into a world of danger and intrigue, she discovers that the very people she is trying to unmask have their own designs on her. The fact that she even knows about their existence puts her life in danger – but could she live with herself if she left the truth hidden forever?

But then she meets Luke Cavenelli, the youngest member of the immortal Cabal. Although he's almost a century old, Luke is kind, debonair, sensual and devastatingly handsome. When she pushes him hard enough, he breaks and gives her the information she craves... and much more.

Love Thy Enemy

ANYA KAREKANOVA #1

***

Anya Karekanova was destined for a life of poverty and misery, until a chance twist of fate sweeps her into the mysterious world of the Immortelle. Now, forty years later, she has become one of them. She is the student and companion of one of her clan's most powerful elders, and even she doesn't fully realise the extent of her new destiny yet.

Anya is the protégée of the dark and violent Slavic Clan, which secretly dominates Russia from behind a veil of secrecy. Anya possesses the bloody ability to perform fleshcraft, which allows her to manipulate living flesh to suit her whims, but that is only part of who she is. Anya Karekanova is a half-breed. While her Siberian blood grants her the Slavic Clan's fleshcrafting abilities, her father's Mediterranean genes link her to the sensual and charismatic Cabal. The Cabal, who use the Power to manipulate the minds of their victims. Half shape-shifter and half empath, Anya must learn to balance the two warring halves of her nature in order to best serve her allies.

Her dual nature makes her an excellent diplomat, which is just what the Clan needs her to be. The time has come to end an ancient blood feud with the Dragon Clans of the Far East, and Anya finds herself in the middle of the negotiations.

Just when things seem to be going so well, an unexpected betrayal turns everything on its head. Suddenly, Anya must fight to defend her oldest enemies – and herself – from a deadly threat.

About The Author

Born in Auckland, New Zealand, Victoria Dreyer began her career in the most peculiar of ways: as the writer and illustrator of graphic novels. Although her ultimate dream was always to become a novelist, she spent many years exploring other mediums before finally returning to the one she felt most comfortable with - the written word.

Ms Dreyer is a voracious reader, and in addition to the post-apocalyptic genre she also enjoys reading and writing science fiction, modern fantasy, and the paranormal romance genres. Her primary works include the *Survivors* series under the moniker V. L. Dreyer, the *Immortelle* series under the moniker Abigail Hawk, and numerous short stories.

She currently resides in the Waikato, a region she fell in love with during the writing of *The Survivors*, with a large collection of books and several very spoilt cats.

www.vldreyer.com
www.twitter.com/VL_Dreyer
www.facebook.com/groups/cheekykeaprintworks/